After a lengthy silence, Gavin said, "We need to discuss what happens next."

Dixie's throat swelled with panic and she swallowed hard. She'd known from the get-go that Gavin was an honorable man and once he learned he'd fathered her baby he'd insist on doing his duty and marrying her.

"Gavin—"

"Dixie—"

"You go first," she said,  marriage proposal.

"I'm not sure what the answer to our predicament is, but I do know that I'm not ready to marry and settle down."

Stunned by his confession, Dixie leaned against the workbench and stared unseeingly at the scattered supplies.

"I want to do right by the baby, so I intend to help you financially."

Her face warmed with embarrassment. What an idiot she'd been to believe Gavin wanted to marry her. Shoving her bruised pride aside, she focused on the positive—he didn't want to be involved in her life.

Dear Reader,

Welcome back to Stagecoach, Arizona! In *A Cowboy's Duty* you'll meet Dixie Cash and her six brothers—each named after a country-and-western singer. You'll get a kick out of the crazy Cash brothers, but the cowboy who will steal your heart is Gavin Tucker. He's a soldier cowboy—a special breed of man who's paid a high price for defending his country.

Many soldiers return from war suffering from post-traumatic stress disorder. Gavin's an adrenaline junkie—feeding his addiction by competing in rodeo. The high he gets from busting broncs gives him the strength to keep running from his past, and as long as the past never catches up to him Gavin is able to keep his PTSD under control. A chance encounter with a female bull rider named Dixie Cash threatens the status quo. When Dixie turns up pregnant, Gavin must face his past before he can seek the future he'd always believed to be out of reach for him.

Dixie and Gavin's love story is about courage, trust and taking a leap of faith. I hope you enjoy accompanying them on their rocky road to Happy Ever After.

For more information about other books in my Rodeo Rebels series, please visit www.marinthomas.com and drop by my blog, *All My Heroes Are Cowboys*, www.marinthomas.blogspot.com, where I always have something to say about the guys who wear Wranglers and Stetsons.

Happy Ever After…The Cowboy Way!

Marin

A Cowboy's Duty

MARIN THOMAS

HARLEQUIN®
entertain, enrich, inspire™

Recycling programs
for this product may
not exist in your area.

ISBN-13: 978-0-373-75418-2

A COWBOY'S DUTY

Copyright © 2012 by Brenda Smith-Beagley

All rights reserved. Except for use in any review, the reproduction or
utilization of this work in whole or in part in any form by any electronic,
mechanical or other means, now known or hereafter invented, including
xerography, photocopying and recording, or in any information storage
or retrieval system, is forbidden without the written permission of the
publisher, Harlequin Enterprises Limited, 225 Duncan Mill Road,
Don Mills, Ontario M3B 3K9, Canada.

This is a work of fiction. Names, characters, places and incidents are
either the product of the author's imagination or are used fictitiously,
and any resemblance to actual persons, living or dead, business
establishments, events or locales is entirely coincidental.

This edition published by arrangement with Harlequin Books S.A.

For questions and comments about the quality of this book
please contact us at CustomerService@Harlequin.com.

® and TM are trademarks of Harlequin Enterprises Limited or its
corporate affiliates. Trademarks indicated with ® are registered in the
United States Patent and Trademark Office, the Canadian Trade Marks
Office and in other countries.

www.Harlequin.com

Printed in U.S.A.

ABOUT THE AUTHOR

Marin Thomas grew up in Janesville, Wisconsin. She left the Midwest to attend college in Tucson, Arizona, where she earned a B.A. in radio-TV. Following graduation she married her college sweetheart in a five-minute ceremony at the historic Little Chapel of the West in Las Vegas, Nevada. Over the years she and her family have lived in seven different states, but they've now come full circle and returned to Arizona, where the rugged desert and breathtaking sunsets provide plenty of inspiration for Marin's cowboy books.

Books by Marin Thomas
HARLEQUIN AMERICAN ROMANCE

*The McKade Brothers
**Hearts of Appalachia
***Rodeo Rebels

To Lauren

When we first met, you were quiet and shy. It wasn't until I got to know you better that I began to see a strong, determined and resourceful young woman. A woman who is not afraid to rely on herself or face the unknown without flinching. Hold fast to your dreams— no matter how long they take to realize or what roads you must travel to achieve them. Believe in yourself, and there will be no limit to what you can achieve.

Things turn out best for the people who make the best out of the way things turn out.
—Art Linkletter

Prologue

"Ready?"

"I'll never be as ready as you are." Dixie Cash grimaced at her friend Shannon Douglas—one of the top female bull riders in the country.

Shannon was forever on the lookout for a rough stock competition and when Five Star Rodeos had agreed to sponsor women's bull riding in three summer events, Shannon had promised to find five women crazy enough to ride with her—Dixie being one of them.

"Here." Shannon held out a bank draft.

"I feel bad taking your money." Dixie shoved the check into the front pocket of her jeans.

"You're worth every penny."

When Shannon had mentioned the rodeos, Dixie had just been hired as a part-time receptionist for a construction company in Yuma. She'd wanted to help her friend but needed money to launch an internet business for her homemade organic bath soaps. Then Shannon had made Dixie an offer she couldn't refuse—a thousand dollars per rodeo.

"Looks like Veronica Patriot has set her sights on Gavin Tucker."

Dixie's gaze followed Shannon's pointer finger. Figures the blonde buckle bunny would target the handsome bareback rider. "If the cowboy knows what's good for him he'll avoid that tramp like the plague." Dixie had run into Gavin—literally—at the Canyon City Rodeo in June when she'd tripped over his gear bag and knocked him to the ground.

"The bull's more of a spinner than a bucker," Shannon said. "Stay centered." The tan Charbray stood docile in the chute, but once freed all hell would break loose.

"Ladies and gentlemen, turn your attention to gate two. Dixie Cash is about to tangle with Bad Mamajamma." The crowd stomped their boots against the bleachers and whistles filled the air.

"If the Cash name sounds familiar it's because Dixie's got six older brothers who rodeo. Earlier today, Merle Cash took third in the saddle bronc competition."

While Shannon and a rodeo helper fished the bull rope from beneath Bad Mamajamma, Dixie pulled on her riding gloves and adjusted her headgear with its protective mask.

Let's get this over with. Dixie straddled the fifteen-hundred pound nuisance, found her grip then nodded to the gate man. The bull pounced for freedom, the first buck almost unseating Dixie. Anticipating a wild ride, she held her breath through the first of two tight spins, squeezing her thighs against the animal's girth.

Bad Mamajamma decided he'd had enough of Dixie and kicked out with extra force. As if she'd been shot from a cannon, Dixie catapulted through the air. She hit the dirt hard, but instinctively curled her body into a ball and rolled away from the bull's hooves. The bull-fighter stepped in front of Bad Mamajamma, affording Dixie an extra second to gain her footing. She ran for the rails and scrambled to safety.

"Well, folks, Dixie Cash gave it her best effort." The announcer discussed Shannon's upcoming ride, but Dixie stopped listening when her boots landed in front of Gavin Tucker.

"Good try," he said.

Try being the operative word. "Thanks." *Brilliant, Dixie. A cowboy with killer looks and nice manners goes out of his way to talk to you and you mumble "thanks"?*

"How long have you been riding bulls?" Gavin asked.

"Started this summer."

A dark eyebrow lifted. "Gutsy gal."

More like crazy. For the life of her, Dixie couldn't find her tongue. Turned out she didn't have to. Veronica Patriot materialized out of nowhere and sashayed her way between Dixie and Gavin. She placed her French-manicured talons on Gavin's chest and thrust her heaving bosom in his face. "Time to celebrate, cowboy."

Dixie despised Veronica. The woman had done a number on her brother Porter—used him to make another cowboy jealous then left him high and dry with a broken heart.

"Sorry, I've got plans." Gavin's soulful brown eyes beseeched Dixie.

"What plans?" Veronica propped her hands on her hips.

Dixie had read her share of silent *help me* messages from her brothers. The look Gavin sent her begged her to rescue him from the clutches of the evil buckle bunny. *What the heck.*

"Gavin and I have a date," Dixie said.

"Pardon?" Veronica frowned.

"That's right." Gavin inched closer to Dixie and the scent of dust and faded cologne went straight to her head. When he rested his arm across her shoulders a little shiver raced down her spine. Gavin couldn't have been more than six feet tall, but her five foot six inches fit perfectly tucked against him.

Veronica's gaze bounced between Gavin and Dixie. "What kind of date?"

"A boy-girl date." Dixie smiled sweetly.

"Honey, a girl like you can't handle a military man."

Dixie had heard that Gavin Tucker had been stationed in Afghanistan before he'd left the army. "What do you think, Gavin? Can I handle you?"

He grinned.

Disgusted, Veronica snorted like a pig and stomped off.

"Thanks." Gavin released Dixie and stepped back.

Wishing he still had his arm around her, she said, "No worries. Veronica can be a pest."

"Are you celebrating later with your lady bull rider friends?"

"Probably."

"I'm heading over to the Spittoon. Maybe I'll see you there."

"Maybe."

Gavin walked off and Dixie couldn't help but think he was exactly the kind of man she'd like to marry someday.

GAVIN STEPPED INSIDE the Spittoon, a bar on the outskirts of Boot Hill, and surveyed the crowd. The place was packed, noisy, and smelled like stale beer, dusty cowboys and easy women. And he hoped Dixie Cash was among the clientele—not that he thought she was a party girl. There was something about the petite, tomboyish cowgirl that drew him. She showed the same courage and spunk as the women he'd worked alongside in the army.

He made his way to the bar, ordered a beer, then found a dark corner away from the crush of bodies. Keeping his back to the wall he searched for the blue-eyed brown-haired girl-next-door. He spotted her at a table next to the dance floor engaged in conversation with her friends. As if she sensed his scrutiny, their eyes connected and Gavin felt the subtle stirrings of arousal.

A former soldier had no business being with a girl like Dixie—that fact in and of itself fed Gavin's desire, and adrenaline pumped through his veins. If there was one thing he was addicted to, it was adrenaline. After six years of living on the edge…living with danger… he was drawn to taking risks. And Dixie Cash was definitely a risk.

"Well, well, well."

Gavin jumped an inch off the floor. *Damn.* How the hell had Veronica Patriot snuck up on him? His temper flared but he counted to ten, as a therapist had once instructed him to do when he felt threatened.

"What happened to your boy-girl date?" The buckle bunny narrowed her eyes.

"Dixie's—"

"Here." Dixie sidled up to Gavin and slipped her arm through his. She stood close enough that her soft breast pressed against his biceps.

"You're not his type." Veronica sneered. "Besides, don't girls like you have curfews?"

"She's right, Gavin. We should leave. It's past my

bedtime." Dixie batted her dark lashes and suddenly Gavin's jeans felt a size too small.

Reminding himself that Dixie's flirting was an act to help him out of a tight spot, he said, "Ready when you are."

"Don't you want a real woman, soldier?" Veronica thrust her bosom out, flaunting her attributes.

After a lengthy glare-down, Veronica stepped aside and Gavin led Dixie across the dance floor and out the door. It wasn't until they were almost to his truck that he realized he still held her hand. He stopped and glanced over his shoulder. Veronica had followed them outside.

"She doesn't give up easily, I'll give her that," Dixie said.

"How would you feel about leaving with me in my truck?"

"I don't know. Can I trust you?"

"Sugar, if I harm one hair on your head, your brothers will hunt me down."

"You're right. I'll go for a ride with you."

Ten minutes later… "She's still following us." Gavin glanced between the road and the rearview mirror. Dixie's stomach growled and he threw caution to the wind. "You up for Chinese takeout? We could eat at the motel. If Veronica sees us go into my room together maybe she'll give up."

"I don't believe that woman knows the meaning of surrender, but I won't turn down a free meal."

Veronica trailed them to the restaurant and then the motel where she parked across the lot, facing Gavin's room. Ignoring their stalker, he and Dixie sat on the king-size bed, ate chop suey and watched the old spaghetti Western, *A Fistful of Dynamite*.

Near the end of the movie, Gavin peeked out the

window. Veronica's Mustang was gone. The woman had finally left him alone. He checked his watch—half past one in the morning. Time to drive Dixie back to the Spittoon so she could be on her way home. "Coast is clear." He turned from the window.

Dixie lay curled in a ball on the bed, her hands folded neatly beneath her cheek, her chest rising and falling in deep, even breaths. In sleep, she appeared innocent and cuddly and he wanted to lose himself in all her sweet goodness. But Gavin didn't dare crawl onto the bed with Dixie and risk falling asleep. He couldn't take the chance he'd experience the recurring nightmare that had followed him home from Afghanistan. He lowered the volume on the TV and made himself comfortable in the chair. He'd gone many nights without a wink of sleep, but the longer he watched Dixie's slumbering body the more exhausted he became.

The sun streaming through a gap in the curtains woke Gavin at the crack of dawn. He wasn't sitting in the chair—he was lying on the bed. Sometime in the middle of the night he'd crawled under the covers. He rolled away from the light and came face-to-face with a wide-awake Dixie.

He held his breath, waiting for her to make the first move—she did. Her lips brushed his, then came back for more. One kiss turned into two…three…then clothes started flying off.

Chapter One

"Hello, Gavin."

The saccharine voice raised a warning flag inside Gavin Tucker's head. Bracing himself, he stepped away from the bucking chute at the Piney Gorge Rodeo and faced Veronica Patriot with a groan. "Veronica."

The woman took buckle bunnying to a whole new level. She'd been pursuing Gavin since he'd joined the circuit back in May after he'd left the army. The middle of August had arrived and the blonde piranha showed no signs of tiring.

Gavin adjusted the spurs on his boots, hoping she'd take his silence as a hint and mosey along. At first, he'd found Veronica's infatuation amusing. He'd become accustomed to pretty women fawning over him whenever he'd worn his military uniform and the same held true for his cowboy getup—Wranglers, boots and a Stetson.

Gavin's ability to attract the opposite sex had come in handy during his furloughs from the army. One look at his combat boots and women had fallen into his bed willingly. He'd honed his survival skills on the battlefield and used them to pick ladies who wanted nothing from him but a good time and a goodbye. A sixth sense told him that Veronica had more on her mind than a quickie.

"You don't appear all that happy to see your biggest fan." She puckered her glossy lips.

A weaker man might tuck tail and run, but Gavin wasn't easily intimidated. "I'm not interested in hooking up." *Ever.*

"Did you and Dixie have a spat?"

Dixie Cash. The petite brunette hadn't crossed Gavin's mind since the morning he'd dropped her off in the parking lot of the Spittoon bar last month. He fought a smile as he recalled the first time he'd caught a glimpse of her—climbing onto a bull named Listless at the Canyon City Rodeo back in June. For an instant he'd seen in her a kindred spirit when Listless had thrown her. Dixie had limped from the arena with a smile on her pixie face as if she'd had the time of her life wrestling fifteen-hundred pounds of orneriness, then she'd stumbled over his gear bag and right into his arms. Her face had burned red and he'd thought her embarrassment oddly sweet.

"Dixie's a friend." *Friend* sounded better than *one-night stand.*

"I can be that kind of friend, too." Veronica's gaze dropped to Gavin's crotch.

His face heated—not because of Veronica's lewd stare. He'd made a mistake when he'd crossed the line with Dixie, yet he'd had no choice but to move on and put that night behind him.

Short of being mean, Gavin said, "Pick another cowboy. I'm not interested in what you're offering."

"When you tire of your little bull rider and decide you want a real woman, I'll be waiting."

One of Gavin's competitors let out a wolf whistle as Veronica strutted off. "I wouldn't complain if she followed me through the copper state."

"Careful what you wish for," Gavin mumbled. Now that he was rid of the annoying buckle bunny he checked the arena for Dixie. He recognized Shannon Douglas mingling behind the chutes with a few of the lady bull riders from the Boot Hill Rodeo, but Dixie was nowhere in sight. She'd probably viewed their one-night stand as a mistake, too, and wanted to avoid running into him.

Turning his thoughts inward, Gavin focused on his ride as he secured his protective vest. After wearing bulletproof gear as part of his military uniform, he felt comfortable in the constricting rodeo garment.

"Welcome to the Piney Gorge Rodeo and Livestock Show!" A thunderous din reverberated through the small outdoor arena. Gavin loved rodeo fans. The men and women were die-hard loyalists to the sport much the way soldiers were dedicated to their units.

"Up next this fine Saturday afternoon is bareback riding! Bareback horses are leaner and quicker than those used for saddle bronc riding and the cowboys sure do take a beating in this event." The announcer paused.

A commotion in the cowboy ready area caught Gavin's attention. The Cash brothers had arrived. Dixie had mentioned that her mother had named her siblings after country-western singers. Right then Johnny, the eldest Cash brother, spotted Gavin. The speculative gleam in the man's eyes unnerved him. Had Dixie told Johnny she'd spent the night with Gavin in his motel room?

He and Dixie hadn't made a big deal over sleeping together. He'd enjoyed—make that had *really* enjoyed— making love to Dixie, but the country girl wasn't his usual type. The things he'd seen and experienced during his years in the military would only contaminate a young woman as pure as Dixie.

Johnny broke eye contact first, and Gavin shook his

head to clear his thoughts. Today he intended to make it to eight. Luck hadn't been with him this summer—the highest he'd placed was fourth. If he didn't get his rodeo act together and pull off a few wins, he'd eat through his savings in no time flat and be forced to find a civilian job. Having to quit the circuit before he was ready was all the motivation Gavin needed to climb onto another wild bronc.

"Ladies and gentlemen, turn your attention to chute number three. Gavin Tucker from Phoenix, Arizona, is about to tangle with Cisco Kid, a bronc known for throwin' cowboys on their heads. Let's see if Tucker can best Cisco Kid."

Gavin blocked out the arena noise as he fussed with his rigging—a heavy piece of leather with a suitcase-like handle attached to it. He flexed his gloved fingers until his grip felt comfortable. A deep breath later, he nodded and Cisco Kid bolted from the chute. Gavin marked out, ignoring the jolting pain shooting through his shoulder caused by the gelding's powerful bucks and lightning speed.

The racket inside Gavin's head quieted as the thrill of the physical torture the horse inflicted rushed through his body. Cisco Kid made a final attempt to spin but Gavin spurred harder and the bronc gave up. Feeling a victory at hand, he relaxed his guard too soon and Cisco Kid tossed him on his arse. Gavin missed the buzzer by one second. Back in the cowboy ready area he gathered his gear. This time he spotted Veronica before she startled him.

"Change your mind about me?" She'd brought a friend along—a redhead with glittery eye shadow. "Candi's up for a little fun," Veronica said.

A threesome? No thanks. Even in his wildest days,

Gavin had never gotten into the kinky stuff. Call him old-fashioned, but one woman at a time was plenty. "Sorry, Veronica—" he swung his gaze to glitter girl "—and Candi. Gotta hit the road." A ride in Wickenburg awaited him.

Candi popped a pink bubble with her chewing gum. "Maybe next time?"

Not a chance. He touched a finger to the brim of his hat then grabbed his bag and left the arena. The sooner he put a few miles between him and those two the better.

An hour down the road, Gavin noticed a billboard advertising Millie's World Famous Hotcakes. He took the exit ramp and pulled into a parking lot crowded with eighteen-wheelers. Gavin found an empty stool at the end of the lunch counter. He rested his hat on his knee and flipped over the white mug in front of him.

A gray-haired waitress named Peggy strolled by with a coffeepot and filled the cup. "Didn't make it to eight?" She offered a sympathetic smile.

"Not today." *Not in a long while.*

"You ain't alone, handsome." Peggy nodded to a table where three cowboys sat, one with an ice pack strapped to his shoulder. "Special's barbecue ribs and corn bread."

"That'll do." While he waited for his meal he mulled over his schedule. The Wickenburg rodeo had a decent purse. If he made the final go-round he'd be guaranteed a share of the prize money. If he lost…he'd head down the road.

A self-admitted rodeo junkie, Gavin got high on the buzz and danger of riding bucking stock. Feeding his adrenaline addiction was his number one priority because it fueled his strength—strength he needed to run from the demons that had followed him home from war.

"HOW WAS THE RODEO?" Dixie asked her brother Johnny when he walked into the kitchen of their grandparents' farmhouse early Saturday evening. She was dying for news about a particular bareback rider, but as soon as her brothers had returned from the Piney Gorge Rodeo they'd gone to their bedrooms to nap.

"Merle made it to the final round before getting thrown." Johnny grabbed a beer from the fridge, then sat at the kitchen table. "Shannon said she hopes your ankle feels better soon."

Dixie's cheeks warmed. She'd discovered she was pregnant two weeks after the Boot Hill Rodeo in July. She'd hated to disappoint Shannon and give up the third thousand-dollar payoff, but she hadn't dared risk the baby's health. She'd told Shannon and the other women about her pregnancy but had asked that they keep it a secret and to tell anyone who inquired after her whereabouts that she'd sprained her ankle—the excuse she'd given her brothers when she'd told them she wasn't competing today.

"Anything else exciting happen at the rodeo?" she asked.

"Depends on what you consider exciting."

"I suppose Veronica Patriot was there." Dixie fussed with the dishes in the sink while contemplating her dilemma—how to glean information about a certain cowboy without drawing her brother's suspicion.

"Veronica's hot on Gavin Tucker's tail." Johnny chuckled. "He got thrown in the first round then split."

"Did Veronica leave the rodeo with Gavin?" Drat, the question slipped from her mouth.

"Why do you care if Tucker went off with Veronica?"

"I don't." After Dixie had spent the night in Gavin's motel room she'd returned to the farm the following morning and confessed she'd stayed at a friend's house because she'd had too much to drink at the Spittoon.

Johnny tossed his empty beer bottle into the garbage and made a beeline for the back door.

"Hey, you promised to fix the shelf in the barn cellar."

"Conway said he'd take a look at it."

Conway Twitty was the fifth born Cash son. All six of her brothers had different fathers. Only Dixie and Johnny shared the same daddy. Her mother had come full circle in her quest for the perfect man and had reunited with her first love, Charlie Smith, only to become pregnant with Dixie. Aimee Cash had never married any of the men she'd slept with, so Dixie and her brothers had taken her surname—Cash.

Dixie and Johnny had the same dark brown hair and blue eyes, which they'd inherited from Charlie. Their brothers had brown eyes and various shades of blondish-brown hair like their mother. "Conway's preoccupied," Dixie said.

"Is he still pouting because Sara broke up with him?"

"I think so." Conway was the handsomest of her brothers and women fawned all over him, which derailed his love life on a regular basis. Each time he found *the one,* another woman would happen along and tempt him to cheat. Then when *the one* caught him two-timing, she'd send Conway packing and her brother would mope like a coon dog left home on hunt day.

"I'll look at the shelf before I leave tonight," Johnny said.

"You and Charlene have big plans?" Charlene was

Johnny's longtime girlfriend. They'd been together six years and Johnny had yet to propose.

"We're going to the movies then back to her place afterward."

None of her brothers brought their significant others to the farm. Paper-thin walls and shared bedrooms prevented any privacy, not to mention having only one bathroom in the house.

"What about you?" Johnny winked. "Got a hot date?"

Right then Dixie's stomach seized and she bolted from the kitchen. She took the stairs two at a time then skidded to a stop in front of the bathroom door. One hand clamped over her mouth and the other pounding the door, she fought the urge to vomit.

"Go away! I'm reading," Porter Wagoner shouted.

Ignoring the bedroom doors creaking open behind her and Johnny's shadow darkening the top of the stairs, Dixie banged her fist harder. *Blast you, Porter.* She spun, intent on dashing outside, but Johnny blocked her escape.

Oh, well. Dixie threw up on his boots.

"Eew!" Willie Nelson chuckled.

"I'll fetch the mop." Merle Haggard leaped over the contents of Dixie's stomach and hurried to the kitchen.

"Sorry." Dixie wiped the back of her hand across her mouth.

"What's all the commotion?" Porter emerged from the bathroom, his eyes widening at the mess covering Johnny's boots.

"Have you been drinking Grandpa's pecan whiskey, sis?" Conway asked.

She ignored her brother's sarcastic joke.

"I see your ankle sprain has miraculously healed." Johnny's gaze drilled Dixie.

"You think it's food poisoning?" Buck Owens asked in his usual quiet voice.

"No. I drank too much coffee today and skipped supper." Growing up the youngest in the pack she'd learned from her brothers how to talk her way out of trouble.

Johnny pointed to the floor. "If all you've had to drink is coffee, what are those white chunks on my boots?"

Merle saved her from having to answer. "Here's the mop," he said, shoving the handle at Dixie.

Her stomach lurched and she tossed the mop back at her brother and fled to the bathroom, slamming the door behind her. Dixie offered up the remainder of her lunch to the porcelain god, then once her stomach settled, she sank to the floor between the toilet and the pedestal sink, too exhausted to face her brothers.

At only five weeks pregnant the morning sickness was hitting her hard. Amazing that her mother had gone through this so many times—by choice. Dixie holed up in the bathroom until the uproar in the hallway faded. Until Buck quit asking if she was okay. Until the shadows of her brothers' boots disappeared from beneath the door. Then she brushed her teeth and gargled with mouthwash. When she emerged from the bathroom, the hallway was empty save for Johnny sitting at the top of the stairs.

Through thick and thin her eldest brother had always been there for her. Dixie sank down next to him on the step. "I'm twenty-three, Johnny. A grown woman. I can take care of myself."

The hurt look in his eyes cut through her. She hated

disappointing him and knew the last thing he wanted was for her to follow in their mother's footsteps.

"Are you pregnant?" he asked.

"Yes." She'd hoped to keep the secret a while longer—until she decided when and how to tell Gavin.

"Who's the father?" he asked.

"I'm not ready to say."

Johnny gaped. "The guy's got a right to know he's fathered a child."

"I'll tell him." *Eventually.* When she was certain she could hold her ground with Gavin. Dixie had plans for the future and wouldn't allow anyone—including the baby's father—to interfere with them.

"Why didn't you tell me the truth this morning when I asked why you weren't going with us to the rodeo?"

"'Cause I knew you'd be mad."

Johnny shoved a hand through his hair, leaving the ends sticking up. "I taught you about birth control."

"We used a condom," she said.

"Not the one I made you put in your purse when you were sixteen, I hope."

She dropped her gaze.

"What the heck, Dixie! That condom was seven years old."

"I know. I know. What does it matter now?"

"Do you plan to keep the baby or do I need to drive you into Yuma to one of those women's clinics?"

"I'm going to keep the baby."

"You sure?"

"Positive."

"Okay then." Johnny stood. "You've got one week to tell me who the father is or I'll make a big stink."

"You better not tell anyone I'm pregnant."

"One week, sis. I'm not letting this guy shirk his

responsibility to you and the baby." As soon as the front door shut behind Johnny, various bedroom doors opened.

"Quit spying!" she shouted, then fled to the barn— her private sanctuary.

Chapter Two

"I'm heading into Yuma. Anyone want to come along?" Dixie asked as she waltzed into the kitchen Wednesday afternoon. Three of her brothers—the unemployed ones—played poker.

"I'll see your five Lemonheads and raise you two." Conway pushed the candy to the center of the table.

"Stupid move, bro," Porter said.

"I'll see your two, little brother, and raise you five." Buck grinned.

"Hey, did anyone hear my question?"

Three heads swiveled in Dixie's direction and her brothers spoke in unison. "What?"

"I've got an appointment with the owner of Susie's Souvenirs in Yuma. Who wants to go with me?"

Conway gaped as if she'd left her brain upstairs in the bedroom. "We're in the middle of a poker game."

"Well, excuse me for interrupting." She grabbed her purse from the counter and stepped onto the wash porch.

"Man, she's touchy," Conway said.

"I heard that!" The smack of the screen door punctuated Dixie's shout.

Halfway to the truck Porter's voice rang out.

"Hey, Dix, wait for me!"

"If you're coming along to pry the name of the baby's father out of me, you might as well stay here," she said when he skidded to stop in front of her.

Porter's smile flipped upside down. "How'd you know?"

Dixie hopped into her 1982 red Ford truck, then cranked the engine and turned on the air conditioner. As soon as her brother shut the passenger-side door, she shifted into Reverse and backed away from the barn. Porter wasn't the brightest member of the Cash clan but Dixie had a soft spot for the brother closest to her age. "They sent you to do their dirty work because you're the youngest—"

"No, you're the baby of the family." He shook his head. "A baby having a baby. That doesn't sound good when you say it out loud."

She glanced in the rearview mirror. Buck and Conway stood on the porch arms crossed over their chests, faces sober.

"I'm not saying who the father is, so you might as well finish your poker game." She stopped the truck.

Porter checked the side mirror. "Nah. I'll go with you."

Chicken.

At the end of the dirt drive, Dixie turned onto the county road and drove west. The trip into Yuma took less than a half hour once they reached the interstate. "You could look for a job while we're in town."

"No one's hiring."

Porter was lazy. She supposed he didn't know any better. His engaging smile and puppy-dog eyes made people want to take care of him and Porter never snubbed a helping hand. "Wouldn't hurt to fill out an application," she said.

"Drop me off at the bowling alley. I'll ask if they're hiring."

And if they weren't, Porter would bowl a few games. When her brother wouldn't stop fidgeting, she asked, "What's the matter with you?"

"How come you didn't tell us you had a boyfriend?"

"I don't have a boyfriend."

His mouth sagged. "You mean, you just…you know…"

"Yes, Porter. I had sex."

"But you've never dated anyone, except for that guy in the high-school band."

"Rick McKee? He wasn't my boyfriend." But Rick had taken her virginity in the backseat of his car the night of the junior prom—an unremarkable experience.

"You're not supposed to have sex with a guy if he's not your boyfriend."

"I bet you've had sex with a girl and you never saw the girl afterward."

"It's different for guys."

"You're such a chauvinist."

"Jeez, are all pregnant women as crabby as you?"

"Sorry." Dixie had kept her emotions bottled up inside her since she'd discovered she was pregnant. If only her grandmother were alive to help her navigate this uncertain time. "I'm scared, Porter."

He turned down the radio. "Scared of what?"

"Of losing my dream."

"What dream?"

"Never mind." She rarely shared her plans for the future with her brothers—mostly because they wouldn't understand. Dixie's dream was really her grandmother's dream. When Ada Cash passed away, Dixie had stood before her open casket and vowed to find a way to make her grandmother's family soap recipes famous.

"I used to have a dream," Porter said.

"What was it?"

"I wanted to be a monster truck driver."

Dixie's dream had a better chance of becoming a reality than her brother's.

"Doesn't matter anymore," he said.

But dreams did matter. Grandma Ada had wanted to sell her soaps to Colgate but Grandpa Ely had insisted she was "plum off her rocker" if she believed a big corporation would buy a few fancy bars of soap from a nobody. Dixie was determined that even in death her grandmother would not remain a *nobody*.

"Why monster truck driving?" she asked.

"Can you keep a secret?"

"Of course." None of her brothers had been able to get her to confess the name of her baby's father and all of them had given it their best shot.

"Remember back in March when I drove up to Phoenix?"

"You said you were helping a friend move into an apartment."

"I lied." Porter lowered his voice. "I went to the Phoenix Monster Truck Rally."

"Why do we have to keep it a secret?"

"Because I did something stupid."

Dixie couldn't believe how *stupid* she'd been to accompany Gavin Tucker to his motel room. If Veronica hadn't hounded the handsome cowboy, Gavin would have never given Dixie the time of day.

She'd had no intention of sleeping with Gavin, but when she'd awoken the following morning to find herself staring him in the eye she hadn't had the power to resist kissing him. When she'd pressed her mouth to his, he'd returned the kiss and the rest had been the stuff of her fantasies.

Porter remained silent, so Dixie prodded him. "Don't leave me hanging. What stupid thing did you do?"

"I wanted to impress a girl I'd met so I told her I was a mechanic for Bob Patton's monster trucks. She asked me why I was in the stands and not with the crew."

"So you snuck your way into the pit area," Dixie said.

"Yeah. Everything was cool until one of the mechanics handed me a wrench and told me to tighten a screw or bolt—I can't remember which—on one of the trucks. I stood there like a dope."

Dixie winced. "What did they do when they figured out you were an imposter?"

"They flung mud balls at me. The TV cameras were playing the video on the JumboTron. The announcer told the fans that this is what happens to boys when they pretend to be monster truck drivers."

Ouch. Wanting to lighten the mood, Dixie changed the subject. "What's everyone doing this weekend?"

"Conway said he's driving to Tucson to visit an ex-girlfriend and Buck and Willie might go with him. Me, Merle and Johnny are heading up to the Growler Stampede."

Dixie wondered if Gavin would be at the stampede. Didn't matter. She'd track him down once she decided how she'd support herself and the baby, while at the same time launch her internet business. She wasn't afraid to tell Gavin he was going to be a father, but she worried what role he'd insist on playing in their baby's life and the possibility that he'd interfere with her entrepreneurial plans.

If Gavin had been a normal cowboy, she'd take for

granted he'd *try* to do right by her. He'd *try* to send her money for the baby. He'd *try* to visit between rodeos. Cowboys *tried* at everything but usually came up short—at least the ones she'd lived with all her life. Gavin was a different breed—a soldier cowboy. She had no experience with soldiers, but she didn't need a high IQ to understand that to be successful in the military a soldier had to be dependable, courageous, loyal and unselfish. The unselfish trait worried Dixie—she didn't want or expect Gavin to change his future plans for her or the baby.

"Why are you shaking your head?" Porter asked.

"I was thinking about how to convince Susie to increase her inventory of my soaps." *Another fib.* They sure slid off her tongue easily these days.

"Don't know why you're gung ho on selling soap." Porter pointed to her stomach. "When you marry the father, you won't have time to make soap."

Not if Dixie could help it. She tried to summon a smidgeon of anger toward Gavin. For what—being handsome? Charming? Behaving like a gentleman? Shoot, he hadn't forced her to get into his truck and drive off with him. No one had put a gun to her head and insisted she shuck her clothes at the Shady Rest Motel. She was the sole proprietor of the mess she was in.

Regardless, she wanted nothing to do with marrying a martyr. The fact that Gavin had apologized profusely after they'd made love was proof he'd regretted the act. Why suffer through the pomp and circumstance of a wedding ceremony when a few months down the road they'd end up divorced—a divorce she'd have to file for because Gavin was too principled to initiate the split.

"Look out!"

Dixie slammed on the brakes. If not for Porter's

warning she'd have blown through the four-way stop on the outskirts of Yuma.

"Didn't realize being pregnant impaired a woman's driving."

"Ha. Ha." Dixie drove six more miles, then swung into the Desert Lanes Bowling Alley. "I'll text you when I leave Susie's," she said.

"Take your time." Porter nodded to a bright yellow Mustang parked near the entrance. "Hailey's working. She lets me bowl for free."

If only Dixie had her brother's charisma she might have talked the online marketing company into setting up her business website for free. When she reached Yuma's historic Main Street, she parked in the lot behind Susie's Souvenirs.

"Susie? It's Dixie," she hollered, stepping into the shop.

"Be right down!" Sandals clacked against the stairs that led to an apartment above the store. Susie greeted Dixie with a smile. "You look good."

"I do?"

The older woman moved closer and studied Dixie's face. "Your skin is glowing." Susie dropped her gaze to the wicker basket in Dixie's hand. "Which one made your complexion so radiant?"

She'd used the same olive soap this morning that she'd washed with the past three years and until today no one had ever used the word *radiant* to describe her.

It's because you're pregnant.

Dixie set the basket on the counter and selected the organic peppermint soap. "This is what I'm using." She held the bar beneath Susie's nose.

"That smells amazing. What's in it?"

"Sunflower, palm, coconut and peppermint oils."

Along with wheat and barley grass, alfalfa, parsley and grapefruit-seed extract. "I also brought along a Christmas soap I'm experimenting with." Dixie handed Susie a star-shaped bar.

"How pretty. I love the threads of red and green that run through the soap." She sniffed. "Pine boughs, fresh fruit and spices. Very nice."

"I was hoping you'd consider using a display instead of leaving the soaps next to the register."

"I won't know if I have room for a stand until I finish stocking the Christmas merchandise," Susie hedged.

Dixie's soaps were available in other stores along Main Street, but Susie's Souvenirs was the most popular tourist shop in Yuma and Dixie made more money here than the other places combined. "Can you find room if I pay you a fifteen-percent commission instead of the usual ten?"

"What else did you bring?" Susie peered inside the basket.

"Eucalyptus and spearmint." Dixie lined up the soaps on the counter. "Lemongrass. Desert Sage. Oats and Spices." Each bar was a unique shape wrapped in colored tissue paper and a frilly ribbon with a hand-stamped label—Dixie's Desert Delights, Inc. $6.99.

"I'll find room for a display."

"Thanks, Susie. I put extra business cards at the bottom of the basket."

"I'll give you a jingle when inventory gets low."

Dixie could only hope she'd sell all forty bars before Christmas.

WHERE THE HELL WAS HE?

Gavin stood in the dark shivering. He knew he was in the desert, because coarse grains of sand pricked his feet. But where in the desert? And what had happened to his weapons? He wore nothing but his sweat-soaked fatigues. The booming sound of a rocket-propelled grenade sent him running, his lungs burning with each gasp of air.

The target exploded in the distance and streaks of bright light lit up the night sky.

Nate! Nate, where are you?

Gavin glanced over his shoulder and a second explosion illuminated the darkness. In that instant of clarity Gavin spotted Nate a hundred yards behind him.

Run, Nate! Catch up!

Something wasn't right—Nate wasn't moving. Gavin turned back, determined to reach his friend, but with each step, his feet sank deeper into the ground as if the desert had turned into an ocean of quicksand.

Nate reached out his hand for help and time passed at a crawl as Gavin pressed forward, muscles burning, sweat stinging his eyes. Fifty yards from Nate another explosion rent the air and suddenly half of Nate disappeared. Gavin stared in horror. Where were Nate's legs?

A thud hit the ground by Gavin's combat boot. He looked down. Half buried in the sand was Nate's leg.

Gavin woke with a start and bolted from the motel bed. He stumbled into the bathroom, ran the cold tap and splashed his face, choking on the water that hit the back of his throat.

Damn it.

He lowered the toilet cover and sat with his head in his hands. He hadn't had a nightmare like this in weeks. Why now?

Maybe he was pushing himself too hard.

Or maybe you're not pushing yourself hard enough.

Whatever the reasons behind his recurring nightmares, as long as Gavin ignored them they'd eventually go away.

"ANOTHER TOUGH NIGHT for Gavin Tucker," the announcer said at the Growler Stampede Rodeo in Growler, Arizona.

Gavin picked himself up and dusted off his jeans, then waved his hat at the crowd as he jogged out of the arena. *Dumb bronc.* Thunder Rolls had tossed him on his head as soon as he'd cleared the gate. Ignoring the twinge in his wrist, Gavin stuffed his gloves into his gear bag.

"Better luck next time, soldier." Mitch Farley, a Colorado rancher approached.

Gavin shook hands with the retired marine. Mitch's son had been stationed with Gavin in Afghanistan. "How's Scott? Still overseas?"

"Yep. He's coming home for Christmas." Left unsaid…*if he doesn't get killed first.*

"What are you doing in Arizona?" Gavin asked.

"Drove down with a neighbor to watch his nephew compete in bull riding." Mitch cleared his throat. "What made you decide not to reenlist?" The older man had spent twenty-five years in the military before taking over the reins of his family's cattle ranch.

Gavin didn't mind discussing his military career with fellow servicemen and women, but he didn't care to share the information with his rodeo competitors. He grabbed his gear and motioned for Mitch to walk with him. "After Nate got killed nothing was the same over there." Nate had been Gavin's best friend. They'd gone to high school together and had joined the army on a whim.

"Is it true one of the villagers you were helping planted the roadside bomb?"

"Yeah." After that day, the goodwill Gavin possessed toward the Afghan people had died a quick death. Gavin thought of the sacrifices he and Nate had made while living in the hostile region. And for what? Nate had given his life and Gavin couldn't shake the dreams that had followed him home.

"You did good work in Afghanistan, son." Mitch clasped Gavin's shoulder. "Don't let one idiot take that away from you."

"After Nate died—" Gavin shrugged off Mitch's touch. The last thing he wanted was pity "—I knew I wasn't going to be any use to the army, so I checked out."

"What about a military position stateside?"

Staying in one place wasn't an option. Keeping on the move was the only way Gavin felt as if he could breathe. "I wanted a change."

Mitch chuckled. "Getting your ass kicked by a wild bronc sure is a change."

"It'll come back to me." Gavin and Nate had competed in rodeos throughout high school and during their military leaves, but admittedly Gavin was rusty and needed a heck of a lot more practice before he'd become competitive.

"You can't rodeo forever. You got a plan B if you end up injured?"

"Not really."

"When you get ready to call one place home, come see me. I could always use a good ranch hand."

The word *home* generated an uncomfortable feeling in Gavin. Settling down was the last thing on his mind. "Nice to know there's a place to hang my hat if I need one."

"Take care." Mitch walked off.

Now what? The next rodeo on Gavin's schedule was in Chula Vista, California—a week from today. He should hit the road but a sixth sense warned him not to be in a rush to leave the Grand Canyon State. His years in the military had taught Gavin to never ignore his instincts.

He chalked up the doom-and-gloom thought to his recent nightmare. He sure in hell didn't want a repeat of that terrifying hallucination. Maybe a drink would settle his nerves and numb his brain while he listened to eight-second stories. The one thing he missed about the army was the camaraderie of fellow soldiers.

"Hey, Waters." Gavin called across the parking lot. "Where's everyone hanging out after the rodeo?"

The calf roper tossed his gear into the back of his pickup. "Mickey's. A few miles east of here."

"Thanks." Gavin got in his truck and checked his cell phone for messages. None. A short time later he parked at Mickey's. Standard cowboy bar—a dump, save for the fancy red door. Neon beer signs brightened the windows, reminding Gavin that he was hungry and thirsty.

The smell of sweat, spilled beer and cigarette smoke greeted his nostrils inside. A thirty-foot bar sans stools stretched along one wall behind which a pair of bald, tattooed bartenders filled drink orders. The rest of the place was crowded with mismatched tables and chairs.

A country-western song wailed from the jukebox as Gavin zigzagged through the maze of rowdy cowboys. "Bud Light." He tossed a five-dollar bill on the bar.

"You win or lose today?" asked the barkeep with a snake tattoo slithering up his neck.

"Lost."

"Tough draw?"

"Not really." He took his beer and strolled through the crowd listening to a country ballad of love gone wrong. Why the lyrics made him think of Dixie he had no idea. He'd regretted making love to her, even though it had been a long time since he'd been intimate with a woman. If only the taste of her bold kiss hadn't drowned out the warning voice in his head.

He'd had a hunch he was the first cowboy she'd ever had a one-night stand with. Thank God she'd had a condom in her purse, because Gavin's protection had been out in the glove compartment of his truck.

He moseyed over to a table near the dartboard where a pair of inebriated cowboys tried to hit the target.

"Hey, Kramer!"

Gavin's senses went on high alert when he recognized the gravelly voice—Johnny Cash. He tuned his ears to the conversation behind him.

"You see my ride?" Cash asked Kramer.

"Yep. Too bad you didn't win."

"Sanders drew a better bronc," Cash said. "You got a minute?"

"Sure. What's up?"

"You were at the Boot Hill Rodeo this past July, weren't you?"

"I bit the dirt on Short Fuse." Kramer chuckled. "Your sister rode a bull in that rodeo, didn't she?"

Gavin tensed.

"Speaking of my sister," Cash said. "Were you at the Spittoon that night after the rodeo?"

"Sure was."

"You happen to see who my sister left the bar with?"

"If I did, I can't remember." Then Kramer asked,

"Wasn't Dixie supposed to ride in Piney Gorge this month?"

"Yeah. She withdrew."

"Your sister plan to do any more bull ridin' in the future?"

"Not for nine months."

The blood drained from Gavin's head and pooled in his stomach, making him nauseous.

Kramer lowered his voice. "You sayin' some guy knocked her up after the rodeo?"

"Yep, that's what I'm saying. I'd like to find the jerk and wring his neck."

"If I hear any rumors, I'll be in touch," Kramer said.

"Thanks. And, Kramer?"

"Yeah?"

"Keep this to yourself."

"Sure. No problem." Kramer headed to the bar and Cash followed.

Gavin didn't give himself time to think; he bolted for the door. Once outside, he cut across the parking lot, hopped into his truck and headed south. After he'd driven an hour he could no longer suppress his anxiety. He pulled off the road, turned on the flashers then left the truck and started walking.

The longer he walked the lower the sky fell and the higher the ground raised, compressing him until each breath felt like he was sucking air through a straw.

Damn his frickin' intuition. If he'd ignored his sixth sense, he'd have been on the road to Chula Vista by now and been none the wiser about Dixie's condition.

Chapter Three

Gavin pulled up to a pump at the Chevron station in Stagecoach. The sudden downpour he'd driven through ten miles back had left behind a rainbow in the sky, and the smell of steamy pavement and wet clay permeated the air. He filled the gas tank, then entered the convenience store.

"Howdy." A slim man with gray whiskers and a toothy smile greeted Gavin. "Passin' through or visitin'?"

"Passing through." Gavin hoped. "I'm looking for the Cash place."

"Was good people...Ely and Ada Cash. Solid, Christian folk." The old man shook his head, dislodging a hank of oiled hair from the top of his noggin. The strand fell across one eye. "A shame, you know."

"What's that?"

"Ely and Ada's only child, Aimee, couldn't keep her legs crossed long enough to find a decent man."

Gavin had heard the gossip on the circuit—that all six Cash brothers had different fathers. He sensed the old man didn't get many customers each day and if he didn't cut to the chase he'd be stuck listening to back-in-the-old-days stories. "There an address for the Cash property?"

The clerk shook his head. "Go back through town and turn right on Route 10. 'Bout eight miles down the road you'll run into the pecan farm."

"Any landmark I should look for?"

"There's a billboard advertisin' Vera's Lounge fer Gentlemen." The geezer chuckled. "Vera ain't runnin' her bawdy house no more, but Peaches, the girl on the billboard, still gives private dances if yer interested."

Gavin wasn't. "Thanks for the directions." He made it to the door before the clerk's voice stopped him. "Don't know what business ya got with the brothers, but don't cross 'em. They'll bring ya down like a pack o' wolves."

Although Gavin's *business* was with Dixie not her brothers, the warning reminded him to watch his back. With each passing mile along Route 10, his confidence slipped. He'd had ample time to mull over the news that Dixie was pregnant. Like a scratched record, his mind replayed the morning-after minutes in the motel room. Dixie wouldn't make eye contact when he'd apologized for letting things get out of hand. He'd guessed that she'd been embarrassed about their lovemaking—now he wasn't sure.

What if Dixie had been in a relationship with another man and they'd had a fight? Then she'd gone to Gavin's motel room and when she woke the next morning, she realized she'd cheated on her partner. Guilty feelings would explain Dixie's withdrawal and the fact that she'd never contacted him about her pregnancy— because her boyfriend was the father of her baby, not Gavin. He sure in hell hoped that was the case. In any event, he wouldn't rest easy until he knew the truth.

And if the baby's yours...

Gavin shoved the thought from his mind when he

spotted the dilapidated billboard in the distance. The sun had faded the sign, but the outline of Peaches's voluptuous curves remained visible. He turned onto a dirt road. Rows of pecan trees for as far as the eye could see escorted him through the property. After a quarter mile, a whitewashed farmhouse came into view. Dixie's truck sat parked out front.

The two-story home was in need of a little TLC. The black shutters could use a coat of paint. The front porch sagged at one end and a handful of spindles were missing from the railing. A swing hung at an odd angle from the overhang and a collection of empty flowerpots sat near the screen door.

Gavin parked next to Dixie's truck and turned off the ignition. He waited for a barking dog to announce his presence but the farm remained eerily quiet. A gray weathered barn with a tin roof sat across the drive. There was no sign of harvesting equipment and Gavin questioned whether the pecan farm was in production anymore. He climbed the porch steps but before he raised his fist to knock, a loud bang echoed through the air. Switching directions he walked to the barn where he found Dixie.

The first sight of her sent an unwelcome spark of excitement through Gavin. There was nothing sexy about Dixie's attire—jeans, a faded oversize Arizona Cardinals T-shirt and rubber gloves that went up to her elbows. She sifted through a large metal tray filled with river rock, then walked to the rear of the barn and dropped a handful of stones into a wooden cask mounted on a brick base. Next, she retrieved several bunches of straw, which she added to the barrel, and she scooped a small bucketful of ash from an old-fashioned potbelly stove with a chimney pipe that vented out the side of the barn.

"What are you making?"

A squawk erupted from her mouth. "Gavin."

His name floated toward him in a breathless whisper. He couldn't recall ever feeling this off balance around a woman. Dixie wasn't a flashy girl with showy attributes, but the aura of warmth that surrounded her attracted Gavin. Her average looks, compassionate blue eyes and long brown hair made him feel safe, encouraging him to let his guard down. The night he'd spent in the motel with her he'd almost forgotten he'd been a soldier. Forgotten where he'd been and what he'd seen.

Forgotten he was broken inside.

He motioned to the workbench crowded with scales, liquid-filled jugs, colored glass bottles that resembled jars from an ancient apothecary shop, potted herbs and tin molds. "Are you and your brothers running a meth lab out of your barn?"

She didn't laugh. "Nothing as exciting as drug-trafficking. I'm making soap."

Soap?

Dixie dumped the remaining ash into the cask. "What are you doing here?" He gave her credit for not beating around the bush.

"Verifying information I heard in a bar."

"Oh?"

"Johnny told a friend you were pregnant." He studied Dixie, searching for the slightest sign he'd hit upon the truth.

Nonchalantly she returned to the workbench and sifted through tin molds. "I am."

Gavin held his breath, waiting for her to confirm he was the father. When she didn't offer any details relief left him light-headed. He'd guessed right—she'd been involved with another man before she'd slept with Gavin. On the heels of relief came an unsettling feeling—disappointment. He was far from old-fashioned but he'd never pegged Dixie as the kind of woman who'd cheat on her man.

For his own peace of mind, he wanted confirmation. "I'm not the father, am I?"

A stare down ensued. Dixie balked first—rubbing her fingers over her eyes.

Tears? "I didn't know lady bull riders cried." His attempt at humor failed miserably. Unaccustomed to dealing with female emotions Gavin gently tugged a lock of her hair, but Dixie kept her watery gaze averted.

"I'm sorry."

Gavin tensed. "'Sorry' meaning…I *am* the father?"

She nodded.

The truth hit him like a fist in the gut. "We used a condom."

"I know," she said, a disgusted note in her voice. "My brother gave me that condom when I was sixteen years old before I went on my first date."

"How old are you now?"

"Twenty-three."

Gavin stifled a groan.

"How was I supposed to know it wouldn't be any good?" She peeled off her gloves and jabbed a finger at Gavin's chest. "You're the guy. You should have had protection in your wallet."

Accepting his share of the blame, he asked, "When did you plan to tell me?"

"Eventually."

"Eventually when?"

"When I was good and ready."

He doubted she'd have been *good and ready* anytime soon. Conflicting emotions raged inside him but
beneath the chaos, he was pleased to learn Dixie wasn't
another Veronica.

Dixie turned her back to Gavin and scooped more
ash into the bucket. This was not how she'd imagined
breaking the news to Gavin that he was about to become a father. She peeked at him beneath her lashes.
He appeared to be taking the news well. Maybe a little
too well—then again when an army man received bad
news, he soldiered on.

"What are you doing with the ash?" he asked when
she dumped the contents of the bucket into the casket.
He didn't want to discuss the baby—fine by her.

"I'm making lye for the soap."

"Isn't lye a dangerous chemical?"

"It is for those who don't know what they're doing."
Years ago a burn on her thigh from the caustic liquid
had taught Dixie the importance of taking safety pre-
cautions when working with the liquid.

"Will breathing that stuff hurt the baby?"

Maybe the baby did matter to him. "I'm careful not
to breathe any fumes." The doors at both ends of the
barn were open and two industrial-size fans circulated
the air.

"You shouldn't make soap until after the baby's
born."

This is why she'd wanted to hold off telling Gavin
about her pregnancy. She didn't want him questioning
her every move or believing he had a say in what she did
or didn't do. Besides, putting off marketing her soaps
for nine months wasn't an option. The company she'd
contracted with to create her business website charged
five-thousand dollars for their service—a thousand dol-

lars less than the normal fee if she paid them in full by the end of November.

After a lengthy silence, Gavin asked, "We need to discuss what happens next."

Dixie's throat swelled with panic and she swallowed hard. She'd known from the get-go that Gavin was an honorable man and once he learned he'd fathered her baby he'd insist on doing his duty and marry her. She'd never admit as much, but making love with Gavin had been an incredible experience and she found the notion of waking up each morning in the same bed with him mighty appealing. She shook her head, clearing the X-rated vision from her mind.

Although she respected Gavin for wanting to do right by his child, he was a soldier used to controlling situations and making split-second decisions in the heat of battle. He called the shots and expected his orders to be followed. There was only one problem—Dixie answered to no one.

"Gavin—"

"Dixie—"

"You go first," she said, bracing herself for a marriage proposal.

"I'm not sure what the answer to our predicament is, but I do know that I'm not ready to marry and settle down."

Stunned by his confession, Dixie leaned against the workbench and stared unseeingly at the scattered supplies.

"I want to do right by the baby, so I intend to help you financially."

Her face warmed with embarrassment. What an idiot she'd been to believe Gavin wanted to marry her. Shoving her bruised pride aside, she focused on the positive—he didn't want to be involved in her or the baby's life.

"I don't want to marry, either," she said, wincing at the crack in her voice. Gavin's expression softened and Dixie lifted her chin. If there was one thing she hated—it was people feeling sorry for her. She'd grown up subjected to sympathetic murmurs from teachers and neighbors who'd known about her mother's loose morals.

And look at you now...following in your mother's footsteps by having a baby out of wedlock.

No. Dixie refused to believe she was anything like her mother. When she'd slept with Gavin she'd had no intention of trapping him into marriage. If anything, her pregnancy made her more determined to become financially independent—the one goal her mother had never achieved.

"Rest assured I'm not walking away from my responsibility to the baby," he said.

Of course not. Gavin was America's hero—just not hers.

"You can count on me to help with medical expenses."

"That won't be necessary. I have health insurance." She and her brothers were covered under the same policy. The income brought in by leasing the pecan groves paid the property taxes, monthly insurance premiums and expenses like utilities, food and the cell phone bill.

"I'll help buy whatever you need for the baby." He nodded as if trying to convince himself of his sincerity. "Crib, high chair...diapers."

If Gavin took care of the baby supplies, Dixie could save the cash she earned from her soap sales in Yuma to pay the rest of what she owed for her website. Accepting help from Gavin would relieve some of the financial pressure, but she feared his contributions might lead him to believe he had a vote in how she raised their baby.

Feeling the strain of pretending their discussion about the baby was everyday run-of-the-mill conversation, Dixie said, "If there's nothing else you wanted..."

He reached past her, his arm brushing her shoulder. The contact sent a zap of electricity through her body. Would a simple touch from Gavin always ignite a powerful reaction in her? He grabbed a Sharpie marker and scribbled a phone number on the bench.

"Call me if you need anything." He pulled out his cell phone, then asked, "What's your number?"

Dixie hesitated. She didn't want Gavin checking up on her, but if she didn't give him the number he'd ask one of her brothers. She recited the digits, warning, "I don't always carry my phone with me."

His dark eyes drilled into her and Dixie got the uncomfortable feeling he could read her mind. "I'll leave a message on your voice mail."

A sudden urge to weep overcame her—*pregnancy hormones*. She walked to the stove and stirred the ashes. *Leave, Gavin.* When a minute passed and he hadn't spoken, she glanced over her shoulder. He was gone. On shaky legs she hurried to the barn door and caught the taillights of his truck.

Dear God, how would she keep her attraction to Gavin from showing if he came and went as he pleased in her life?

She glanced at his phone number, startled by the stack of twenty-dollar bills resting on the worktable.

Gavin's first child-support payment.

GAVIN MADE IT AS FAR AS the end of the drive on Dixie's property before hitting the brakes. Three pickups pulled onto the one-lane dirt road. The Cash brothers had returned from the rodeo in Growler.

Johnny drove the first truck and kept on coming, stopping inches from Gavin's bumper. He made no move to back up, which meant Gavin had to back down. Keeping his gaze on the rearview mirror, he shifted into Reverse and pressed the gas pedal. Once he reached the farmhouse he shut off his truck. The Cash brothers circled their vehicles like a wagon train.

Gavin's senses were on high alert as he stepped from the truck. He and the brothers faced off. A sweat broke out across his brow. The cotton material beneath his armpits dampened and his blood pumped through his veins like a white-water rapid.

"What's going on?"

Dixie's voice penetrated Gavin's military fog and the buzzing in his ears weakened as she marched across the yard, arms swinging.

"What's Tucker doing here?" Johnny asked.

Gavin held his tongue, deferring to Dixie to inform her siblings that he'd fathered her baby.

"He's interested in my soaps," she said.

Did she really think her brothers would buy the lie?

Johnny moved closer, crowding Gavin's personal space.

One...two...three...

"Since you drove all this way to check out my sister's soaps, the least we can do is invite you to supper."

Four...five...

Johnny stepped back and Gavin sucked in a deep breath, the lungful of oxygen easing his anxiety. He glanced at Dixie. Her eyes pleaded for him to leave. "I'll stay."

"Willie, grab some beers." Johnny nodded to the porch. "Take a load off, Tucker."

An hour later, Merle took the half-empty beer bottle from Gavin and handed him a fresh one. "For a soldier, you drink like a sissy," he said.

Gavin wasn't going to be bullied into getting drunk so he'd spill his guts about his relationship—whatever it was—with their baby sister. He checked his watch—5:00 p.m. and no one had fired up the grill. He set aside his beer and stood. "I need to hit the road." A beefy hand on his shoulder pushed him down on the porch step.

"Dixie, when are the burgers gonna be ready for the grill?" Johnny called.

The screen door smacked against the house and Dixie shoved a platter of raw meat at Johnny. "Quit yelling." She whapped his chest with a spatula then retreated inside the house.

Porter appeared with a sack of charcoal and dumped the entire bag into the belly of the large Weber grill. He then stuck his hand through a hole in the latticework covering the lower half of the porch and pulled out a large can of lighter fluid. After soaking the briquettes, he tossed a lighted match into the cooker. A fireball shot into the air.

"Hey, Tucker," Merle said. "Why'd you leave the army?"

"After my buddy Nate Parker died I didn't want anything to do with the military." Following Nate's death Gavin had been forced to attend several sessions with a shrink. He'd decided if there was any hope of putting his time in Afghanistan behind him he had to walk away from everything associated with the military.

Johnny spoke. "Never knew you and Parker were friends."

"Parker's story hit all the TV stations throughout the state," Merle said. "It'd been a while since Arizona had lost one of its own."

"We were up in Flagstaff at a rodeo the weekend the news broke," Johnny said. "There was a moment of silence for Parker."

"Nate would have appreciated that."

"You should have stuck to soldiering, Tucker." Willie snickered. "You suck at bareback riding."

"Rodeo suits me fine."

"I'm sorry about Parker," Buck chimed in.

Gavin missed the good old days when he and Nate had traveled the circuit together. As the only child of a single mother, Gavin thought of his army buddy as a brother. "Nate was a damned good soldier. He didn't deserve to die." Didn't deserve to have his body blown into pieces.

Merle went inside, then returned a minute later with a guitar. He played "Song for the Dead" by Randy Newman—a tribute to a fallen solider. Merle's baritone voice was easy on the ears and Gavin's thoughts drifted to the good times he'd shared with his childhood friend. When the song ended, he said, "That was nice. Thanks."

Johnny motioned for Gavin to follow him to the cooker. "What's going on between you and my sister?"

Gavin suspected the eldest Cash brother believed he'd fathered his sister's baby. "We're just…friends."

The look in Johnny's eyes called Gavin a liar. "Where's your home these days?"

"Nowhere in particular. I'm not itching to put down roots."

"We all—" Johnny nodded to his brothers on the porch "—grew up hearing people call our mother a tramp, a slut and a gold digger."

Gavin knew where Johnny was heading with this speech.

"Dixie's not like our mother. She doesn't deserve being called names."

"I've never believed Dixie was anything but a nice girl."

"Good. 'Cause I better not hear one bad word about her on the circuit."

"Mind if I ask you a question?" Johnny had piqued Gavin's interest about the Cash family.

"Fire away."

"Is it true you and your siblings all have different fathers?"

"Only Dixie and I share the same father."

"Do your brothers keep in touch with their fathers?"

"Nope. What about your family?"

"I'm an only child. My mother lives in Phoenix and works for the parks and recreation department."

"I can't imagine growing up an only child."

"No fights for the bathroom."

The joke fell flat. Shoot, the soldiers in Gavin's army unit had thought he was a funny guy.

"You plan to make rodeo a career?" Johnny asked.

"For the time being."

"Willie's right—you stink at rodeo."

"You're not so great, either." Gavin changed the subject. "How long has Dixie been making homemade soap?"

"Since she was ten or eleven. Dixie sells the bars in

tourist shops in Yuma." Johnny lowered his voice. "Between you and me…she's got this harebrained idea she can sell our grandmother's soap online."

Gavin was impressed with Dixie's ingenuity but worried with the baby coming that now wasn't the best time to start up a new business.

A movement near the porch caught Gavin's attention. Dixie spread a plastic cloth over a picnic table in the yard. She made several trips in and out of the house for plates, glasses, condiments, buns and pitchers of lemonade and iced tea. Gavin was astonished that none of her brothers offered to help. Instead, the men sat on their backsides, jawing. A newborn would bring added stress to Dixie's life—a life already busy with soap-making, starting a new business and catering to six grown men.

You're no better than the Cash brothers—you're walking away from Dixie.

"Burgers are done!" Johnny shouted.

The brothers raced to the picnic table and Dixie motioned for Gavin to sit at the opposite end from her. He pulled out his chair and there resting on the seat was the cash he'd left Dixie in the barn. He glanced down the table and her steely-eyed glare told him exactly what he could do with his money.

Shove it up his you-know-what.

Chapter Four

Not again.

Gavin halted in his tracks when he caught sight of Conway and Willie Cash jawing with the cowboys near the bull chutes. The San Carlos Roundup Rodeo took place the first weekend in September—two weeks after he'd learned about Dixie's pregnancy—and darned if he hadn't run into one or more Cash brothers at the events he'd competed in. He presumed the men concluded that he'd knocked up their baby sister and weren't letting him out of their sight.

Too bad Gavin couldn't blame his dismal performances on the constant scrutiny. Instead, impending fatherhood disrupted his focus. Dixie was close to eight weeks pregnant and thoughts of her and the baby wandered through his mind 24/7. How was Dixie feeling—did she have any food cravings? Had she gained weight? What about morning sickness—did she suffer from that? The questions hammered his brain nonstop making him irritable and edgy.

Ignoring Dixie's siblings, Gavin focused on the bronc he'd drawn for today's competition. Jigsaw had a proven track record of bucking off experienced riders. The rodeo announcer introduced the cowboys competing in the bareback event, offering stats on the better athletes. Gavin was described as the former soldier turned cowboy, which drew the loudest applause. He was humbled by the fans' heartfelt appreciation for his service to their country. Once each weekend he felt like a hero even though he was the furthest thing from a Caped Crusader.

"Let's see if Tucker can end his losing streak," the announcer said.

Gavin climbed the chute rails and eased onto Jigsaw's back. *Keep your balance.* An image of Dixie collecting ash from the potbelly stove in the barn flashed before his eyes.

Stay focused.

Fearing Dixie would disrupt his thoughts again, Gavin ignored his chute routine and nodded to the gate man. The door swung open, and Jigsaw demonstrated his superiority in the sport. The bronc's rump twisted in the middle of a buck. Gavin lost his rhythm and his spurring became choppy. Then Jigsaw spun in a tight circle and Gavin was history. He sailed through the air and landed on his belly, the hard ground knocking the wind from him. The pickup men attempted to corner the bucking horse, but Jigsaw evaded capture.

The earth beneath Gavin shook and instinctively he rolled left. Too late—Jigsaw's hoof grazed his shoulder and a searing pain shot through the muscle. As if he'd made his point, the bronc trotted from the arena without an escort. Gavin struggled to his feet, his fingers tingling as numbness spread through his arm.

"Close call." Willie Cash met Gavin when he returned to the cowboy ready area.

Arm hurting like hell, Gavin wasn't in the mood to spar with the Cash brothers.

"Where's your next rodeo?" Conway asked.

"Check with your spies…they'll know where I'm riding."

The brothers spoke in unison. "What spies?"

"Your brothers. One of you always turns up wherever I ride."

Conway grinned. "Johnny said we're not to let you out of our sight."

Gavin wouldn't have a moment's peace until he did right by Dixie. He grabbed his gear, wincing at the throb in his shoulder. "See you at the next go-round." He stopped short of leaving the chute area when he heard Shannon Douglas's name over the loudspeakers.

"Folks, we got a special treat tonight before we kick off the men's bull riding competition. For those of you who haven't heard, Shannon Douglas from Stagecoach, Arizona, has been riding bulls since high school. She competed in three Five Star Rodeo events this past summer and earned a sponsorship from Wrangler."

The JumboTron flashed images of Shannon at the rodeos in Canyon City, Boot Hill and Piney Gorge. Gavin moved closer to the cowgirl's chute and watched her wrap the bull rope around her hand.

"Shannon's about to tangle with Persnickety, a bull from the famed Red River Ranch in Oklahoma."

The chute door opened and Persnickety launched himself into the arena. Shannon's compact body undulated with the bull's explosive bucks and sharp spins. Gavin glanced at the JumboTron…5…4…3…

Persnickety reared and Shannon lost her seat, sliding off the back of the bull. As soon as she landed on the ground she scrambled to her feet and ran for the rails.

"Too bad, folks. I thought Shannon might best Persnickety but not today!"

Gavin turned to leave when he heard his name called. Shannon jogged toward him.

"You almost had that bull," Gavin said.

"I'll get him next time." She sucked in a deep breath. "I haven't been back to Stagecoach in over a month. How's Dixie feeling?"

Gavin supposed Dixie had told Shannon about her pregnancy when she'd scratched at the Piney Gorge Rodeo. "Fine, I guess."

"You guess? Aren't you keeping in touch with her?"

Gavin didn't care to go into detail about his and Dixie's relationship—whatever it was. *You're about to have a baby together and you can't define your relationship?* "I saw Dixie a couple of weeks ago and she looked good." More than good.

Shannon lowered her voice. "She's going to have the baby, right? Or did she…?"

Stunned, Gavin couldn't respond. Dixie having an abortion had never crossed his mind, but that didn't mean it hadn't crossed Dixie's.

"Gavin?"

"I gotta go." He left the arena and cut across the parking lot to his truck. He stowed his gear in the backseat, then started the engine and cranked the air-conditioning. While the cab cooled, he grabbed his cell phone from the glove compartment and checked messages. Nothing.

Call her.

When Dixie had returned his money, the message had been loud and clear—don't interfere.

At first Gavin had been relieved Dixie had expected nothing from him, but the long hours of driving between rodeos had left him with too much time to think. He'd reflected on his father—a deadbeat dad who'd never been there for his son. Once Gavin had joined the military he'd lost all contact with his father and to this day didn't know his whereabouts.

Dixie had grown up without a father, too. Gavin had the power to make sure their child had a father—that is if Dixie hadn't taken matters into her own hands.

Gavin hit three on his speed dial. "Hey, Mom. Gotta minute?"

"What's wrong, honey? You never call on Saturday nights."

"I need some advice."

"Sure." She laughed. "I love telling you what to do."

There was no easy way to say it. "I got a girl pregnant."

A sigh filled his ear. "How old is she?"

"Twenty-three."

"Poor girl."

Poor girl? Dixie, the bull rider turned soap maker was not a *poor* girl.

"What are you going to do?" his mother asked.

Gavin wasn't marriage material, but how could he walk away from Dixie when he'd seen firsthand how tough it had been for his mother to raise a child on her own.

Dixie isn't alone. She has six brothers.

Admittedly his career in the military had left Gavin with rough edges, but he wasn't so sure the Cash brothers would be better role models for his son or daughter. The *uncles* would turn the kid into a hooligan.

"I offered money to buy things for the baby but she threw the cash back in my face."

"You're not marrying this girl?"

"She isn't interested in marriage."

"You mean you proposed and she said no?" When

he didn't answer his mother asked, "What's scaring you, honey?"

"I'm not ready to settle down." Gavin was an emotional and mental mess. He was in no shape to be in a committed relationship. In order to function normally when he'd returned from Afghanistan he'd made sure to keep emotionally distant from the world around him. He doubted Dixie wanted to marry a man who acted as though he didn't care about anything.

After leaving the military, Gavin had promised himself no long-term commitments and raising a child was sure in heck a lasting stint. Dixie was stubborn, bossy and independent. He worried that a marriage between them would be doomed to fail.

"What's this girl's name?" Gavin's mother asked.

"Dixie."

"That's cute. Where does she live?"

"Stagecoach."

"Never heard of the place."

"It's a small town outside of Yuma. Her mother's dead and her father's out of the picture but she has six brothers."

"What do her brothers say about the situation?"

"The eldest expects me to marry Dixie and the rest have me trained in their crosshairs."

"The more I learn about Dixie and her family the more I like."

"Then you'll appreciate hearing that she rode bulls in a couple of rodeos this past summer and she makes homemade organic soap."

"Intriguing. Is she pretty?"

"Sure."

"She must be nice if you've spent time with her."

Dixie was nice. She was kind and compassionate and

had been willing to help him out of a tight spot when Veronica Patriot had put a bull's-eye on his chest.

"No one can force you to marry, but whatever you decide I'm here if you need to talk."

"Thanks, Mom. Everything okay on your end?"

"Barney and I have a new neighbor."

Barney was the five-year-old bulldog Gavin had given to his mother the Christmas before he'd shipped out on his first military assignment.

"Ricardo owns a Chihuahua named Chica and we've been taking the dogs on walks together."

"Does Ricardo know your son is a former army soldier?" Sylvia Tucker was forty-four years old and very pretty, which made Gavin all the more protective of her.

"Don't go all military on me, young man. Ricardo is a gentleman and we're just friends."

Gavin heard the doorbell chime in the background.

"Keep me posted on what you and Dixie decide to do."

"Mom?"

"What?"

"I don't want to disappoint you."

"You're a good man, honey. You'll figure out what's best for everyone."

Gavin tossed the phone onto the seat. Was marriage the answer for him and Dixie? The old-fashioned way to deal with an unplanned pregnancy was a hasty wedding, but a legal document wasn't necessary for Gavin's child to use his last name or for Gavin to be involved in his or her life.

Think, man. Think.

Gavin had survived his tour in Afghanistan. Figuring his way out of this mess with Dixie should be a piece of cake.

Or not.

"HEY, DIXIE, IT'S SUSIE. Could you drop off more of your soaps?"

"You sold out my supply?" Dixie set aside the utensils she'd been cleaning in the barn.

"A guy came in today and purchased every last one. Said he was putting them in goody bags for a corporate shindig."

Dixie grabbed a marker and wrote *corporate goody bags* next to Gavin's cell number. What a great promotional idea for her online business. "Did the man say where he was from?"

"Nope." Susie laughed. "I thought he was pulling my leg."

"Why's that?"

"He was dressed like a cowboy."

Cowboy? Dixie's excitement fizzled. "What did he look like?"

"Like all the others—Stetson, Wranglers, boots. He smelled nice. Hmm…maybe he wasn't a real cowboy."

"Describe his hair." Dixie's brothers wore their hair on the long side because they preferred spending money on rodeo entry fees rather than barber visits.

"Short and he was clean-shaven. He had nice teeth, too."

Gavin.

He hadn't phoned her—not that she expected him to, although part of her had hoped he'd check in with her. After her first doctor's appointment a week ago she'd considered informing him that the baby was fine, but she'd chickened out.

What did Gavin intend to prove by buying her soap inventory?

You threw his money back in his face.

"There'll be lots of tourists in town for the start of the Scarecrow Festival tomorrow," Susie said.

"I'll pack up a basket of soaps right now. See you soon." Dixie ended the call and went into the storage room at the rear of the barn. She opened a door in the floor then flipped on the light switch and descended the stairs. Instead of dank, damp earth the cellar smelled like utopia—a mixture of nature's best scents.

She remembered the adoring expression on her grandmother's face when Grandpa Ely had installed electricity in the barn. No longer had her grandmother been forced to use kerosene lamps when she'd worked late at night.

Dixie gathered the remaining twenty-seven bars and left the cellar. She didn't care for the way Gavin had wanted to make his point—that he intended to support the baby whether she wanted his help or not.

Maybe she'd acted childishly when she'd returned the cash he'd left in the barn, but he'd bruised her pride when he'd insisted he wasn't ready to marry. *Next time take his money and save yourself the aggravation.*

Dixie didn't leave a note before she drove to Yuma— all six of her brothers had left before sunup for who-knew-where and who-knew-how-long. As she drove down the dirt road, she contemplated being a single mom. Not only would she face financial struggles raising her baby but becoming pregnant had taken away her childhood dream of marrying. Eligible men did not chase after hardworking single moms, and in no way was Dixie taking a page from her mother's book—how to land a man and lose him in less than nine months.

Aimee had been a pleaser—a woman who'd gone to great lengths to make a man feel appreciated and valued. Men had preened in her presence because she'd made them feel worthy—even when they'd been unemployed or drunk. In the end, what had drawn men to Aimee had also sent them fleeing. She'd inflated a man's self-esteem to the point where he'd believed he'd risen above her and deserved a better woman. Off he'd run, leaving her high, dry and pregnant.

Dixie knew some guys wouldn't object to raising another man's child, but she refused to make a fool out of herself to attract one. Her brothers were prime examples of males expecting women to flatter them at every turn. Dixie blamed her siblings' cocky attitudes on their mother, who'd insisted at every turn that her sons were the handsomest young men in all of Arizona. However, when it came to Dixie, her mother had said, "Don't worry, child, you'll grow out of your tomboy looks."

For the most part her mother had been right—the sharp angles of Dixie's face had softened over time but she wasn't and never would be the beauty her mother had been. Combine her average looks with having a child out of wedlock and her prospects of marrying Prince Charming were slim to none.

At the end of the drive, Dixie turned left onto the rural road. She traveled less than a mile when the steering wheel locked up on her. "Damn." She wrestled the wheel, managing to guide the car onto the shoulder where she shut off the engine and set the emergency brake. She didn't know a lot about engines but guessed the truck was leaking power-steering fluid.

The weather channel had forecasted 101 for the day's high. She didn't dare risk the last of her inventory melting into a puddle of goo. She placed the basket of soaps in the shade on the floor then got out and wiggled beneath the truck to check for leaks.

Amber-colored fluid formed a puddle on the ground beneath the engine. *Wonderful. Frickin' wonderful.*

Instead of using the three hundred dollars waiting for her at Susie's shop to help pay for her website, she'd have to use the money for truck repairs.

THE TRUCK PARKED ON THE shoulder of the road near the turnoff to the Cash pecan farm looked suspiciously like the red Ford Dixie drove. Worried it might be hers, Gavin made a U-turn and parked behind the vehicle. He walked up to the passenger side and poked his head through the open window. A basket of Dixie's soaps rested on the floor.

Where was she? He shielded his eyes from the sun and looked down the road. Had she found shade beneath a scraggly bush or had she hiked back to the farm? She wasn't crazy enough to walk in hundred-degree heat while pregnant, was she?

Don't answer that.

"Dixie!"

Maybe a passing motorist had offered her a lift. Apprehension exploded into a full-blown anxiety attack as his mind invented all kinds of scenarios—none comforting. What if she passed out from heat exhaustion and lay in a ditch? Or worse, what if the person who'd given her a lift had abducted her and taken her across the border?

The fear gathered steam inside Gavin and triggered a flashback of Nate's death. Gavin's heart pounded so hard he thought the organ would burst through his chest wall. Breaking out in a sweat, he struggled to take deep breaths but only managed to wheeze. In an attempt to block out the flying body parts, Gavin closed his eyes, but the action only intensified the vision and he stopped breathing all together when an image of Dixie bound and gagged in the trunk of a strange car flashed through his mind. He opened his mouth but terror smothered his vocal chords and her name came out in a gasp. Cursing, he summoned his inner strength and shouted, "Dixie!"

"I'm right here."

Gavin spun, then stumbled in shock. He slammed his palm against his chest, jump-starting his stalled heart.

Breathe. She's okay.

"What's the matter?" Dixie took a step toward Gavin but froze when he backed up.

The relief Gavin felt that nothing evil had befallen Dixie was so acute his chest physically ached. He opened his mouth to suck in air but his lungs drew in a gasp.

"You're scaring me, Gavin."

Shit. He was scaring himself. "I'm fine." He rubbed his brow, swallowing a curse when he noticed his trembling hand.

The only explanation he could come up with for his over-the-top reaction was that he cared about Dixie more than he'd believed.

She's pregnant with your baby—it's natural to be concerned about her. Worry was fine but anything more was out of the question—for her sake and his.

Feeling as if his insides had been sliced open with a hunting knife, Gavin pulled himself together and studied Dixie's flushed face and perspiring brow. Sweat stains marked her T-shirt and the strands of hair that escaped her ponytail stuck to her damp face and neck. "What happened to the truck?"

"It's leaking power-steering fluid. I was under the truck checking the engine when you drove up."

"You have no business crawling on the ground in

your condition. What if another vehicle had rear-ended the truck? You could have been killed." He spread his arms wide. "And why are you out in this heat? You should be at home resting in front of a fan."

Dixie wiped her brow, the gesture propelling Gavin in action. Taking her arm he escorted her to his truck. After starting the engine, he directed the air-conditioning vents toward her face then handed her a water bottle from the cooler in the backseat. "Drink."

"Yes, sir." Dixie guzzled the water. "Would you please fetch the basket from the truck? I don't want the soaps to melt."

Gavin did Dixie's bidding, setting the basket on the backseat.

"I've got a bone to pick with you," she said after Gavin got into the truck.

"Pick away." Gavin didn't think—he just did it—and brushed a strand of sweaty hair off her cheek. He swore he heard her sigh but it must have been his imagination, because her eyes flashed with anger.

"What point did you hope to make by buying every last one of my soaps from Susie's Souvenirs?"

"She told you?"

"Susie said a cowboy purchased them for corporate goody bags." Dixie quirked an eyebrow. "Unless I'm plum dumb, rodeos don't qualify as corporate events and cowboys don't care to shower with lavender-oatmeal soap."

"You wouldn't take my money, so you left me no choice."

She crossed her arms and tapped the toe of her shoe on the ground.

"We'd better figure this out right now, Dixie, because I'm not going to play the money game with you.

You're carrying my child and I have an obligation to support—"

"I'm not an obligation!"

Bad choice of words. Gavin reined in his temper. In a neutral voice he asked, "Where were you headed before your truck broke down?"

"Yuma. The Scarecrow Festival kicks off tomorrow and I was taking Susie the rest of my supply." She leaned over the seat and grabbed the shopping bag filled with the soaps Gavin had purchased from Susie's store. "Instead, I'll return these."

After checking the mirrors he pulled onto the road. When they reached Stagecoach, he asked, "Would you like to stop for a bite to eat before driving the rest of the way into Yuma?"

"No, thanks."

Gavin turned on a country music station and focused on the lyrics of the song in an effort to cleanse his memory of the terror he'd experienced a short while ago. When he felt close to normal he glanced across the seat, expecting to find Dixie snoozing. Instead, she gazed out the window in a trancelike state.

"I went to my first doctor's appointment a few days ago." She kept her eyes averted. "They did blood tests and everything checked out fine."

His fear that Dixie might have changed her mind about having the baby died a quick death. "You're eight weeks now?"

"About."

"Did the doctors give you a due date?"

"March 24, but she said first babies are usually late."

March twenty-fourth. Gavin could barely think ahead to his next rodeo never mind the birth of his child. In the military he'd kept his thoughts in the present and had never jinxed himself by contemplating the future. Too many guys made plans then ended up wounded or dead.

"Gavin?"

"Yeah?"

"If you really want to help support the baby, then you can loan me a thousand dollars."

The amount didn't faze Gavin—he had a decent-size savings account. "Your insurance didn't cover the cost of the doctor's visit?"

"I don't need the money for bills. I need cash to pay the marketing company that's designing my website."

"They're charging you a thousand dollars?"

"Five thousand. I saved two grand on my own, then Shannon Douglas offered to pay me a thousand dollars per rodeo to compete in bull riding events this past summer. I would have had five grand by now but when I discovered I was pregnant I withdrew from the Piney Gorge Rodeo in August."

Dixie had taken a heck of a chance for a measly two thousand dollars. Her recklessness worried Gavin. What kind of a mother would she be if she had no qualms about risking life and limb for a few bucks?

"I'd pay you back a little at a time," she said.

"If I become an investor in your company does that mean I have a vote in your businesses practices?"

She stiffened. "Absolutely not. I make all the decisions. Your money would be a loan not an investment."

"Is now the right time to be starting a new business?"

"Why not? There's no stopping the baby from coming."

"Exactly. The baby should be your main focus, not selling soap."

"You expect me to park my butt in a chair and do

nothing but read magazines and drink lemonade all day?"

Yes. "No, but slaving over hot soap molds and working with dangerous chemicals isn't good for the baby." *Or you.*

She snorted. "Now I understand why you get along with my brothers—you're a chauvinist."

"Am not. I think it's great that you have aspirations to start your own company."

"But?"

"It would be best if you waited until a few years after the baby's born."

"A few years?"

"Three or four. Once the kid's in school—"

"How interesting that I have to sacrifice my plans to care for the child, while you do as you please."

Gavin opened his mouth to object but couldn't think of a damn thing to say in his defense.

"Whether you approve or not, I intend to work while I'm pregnant and continue working after the baby's here."

Dixie wasn't backing down and Gavin reluctantly admired her spunk. "Okay. I'll give you the thousand dollars."

"You'll *loan* me the money. I'm paying you back— with interest."

Investing in a soap company wasn't the way Gavin pictured supporting his child, but if it got the job done, who was he to complain?

Chapter Five

"Your truck's gone," Gavin said, waking Dixie from her nap in the front seat. After they'd eaten at a diner outside of Yuma, she'd slept the rest of the way to Stagecoach.

"One of my brothers probably towed the truck to the farm—" Dixie yawned "—when they got home from the rodeo."

Hair mussed and eyes swollen from sleep, she looked like a pixie. An image of a little girl with brown pigtails popped into Gavin's mind and he wondered if Dixie was carrying his daughter—not that he had a preference regarding the child's sex.

"Is the farm in production anymore?"

"Yes, but after my grandparents died and my brothers began rodeoing, we leased the acreage to a company, which operates other farms in the area."

"How long is your contract with the company?" Gavin asked.

"Four years."

"What will you do with the property if you can't lease the land anymore?"

"This is home and I speak for my brothers when I say that we'd never sell the land or the house."

"Small house for seven people."

"That's for sure. Sharing a bathroom with six smelly men is not fun."

Gavin pulled up to the farmhouse and surveyed the trucks parked helter-skelter in the yard. "I don't see your pickup."

"Maybe they took it to Troy Winter's place. He fixes cars for real cheap." Before Dixie had a chance to un-snap her seat belt, the porch door opened and all six Cash brothers walked outside—none of them smiling.

Gavin got out of the truck, rounded the hood and held open the passenger-side door for Dixie.

"We thought you'd been abducted when we found your Ford stranded on the side of the road," Johnny's said.

"Yeah, sis," Willie spoke up. "How come you didn't call? We left messages on your cell phone."

"Sorry." Dixie didn't sound a bit apologetic. "Gavin happened to drive by and rescued me."

"You're a regular knight in shining armor, aren't you, Tucker?" Merle said.

"Where have you been?" Johnny asked when Dixie stopped in front of the porch.

"Delivering inventory to Susie's."

Johnny opened his mouth but Dixie cut him off. "Susie sold out of my soaps and with the festival to-morrow I didn't want to miss an opportunity to make more money." She climbed the steps, pausing when the group blocked her path. "Move. I have to use the bath-room." Her brothers parted like the Red Sea.

As soon as Dixie disappeared inside the broth-ers switched their focus to Gavin. "We need to talk, Tucker." Johnny trotted down the steps and headed to-ward the barn. Feeling as if he was being led behind the woodshed for a whipping, Gavin trailed the eldest Cash sibling.

"What are your intentions toward my sister?" Johnny stopped inside the barn. He crossed his arms over his chest and leaned against the workbench.

"My intention is to do the right thing, but your sister isn't cooperating."

"You proposed to Dixie?"

"No!"

Johnny's eyes rounded.

Gavin shoved a hand through his short-cropped hair. "We're not at a point in our relationship where we're ready to discuss marriage."

"You two passed that point back in July."

"Has Dixie said anything about wanting us to marry?"

"Are you kidding? She still won't say who the baby's father is." Johnny narrowed his eyes. "But we both know who put a bun in my sister's oven."

Jeez. He didn't need to make what Gavin and Dixie shared sound dirty.

"My brothers and I are the only family Dixie has and our job is to look out for her." Johnny paced between the bench and the potbelly stove. The man was wound up tighter than a yo-yo.

"I expect you to marry my sister and make a decent woman out of her."

Gavin was used to giving orders not taking them. "This isn't the eighteen-hundreds, where women are ostracized for becoming pregnant out of wedlock."

"Our family has been talked about and ridiculed all of our lives because of our mother's wild ways. I won't allow Dixie to suffer any more than she already has."

Gavin hated that people might mistreat Dixie because she had a baby out of wedlock, but he feared the one thing guaranteed to protect her against public condemnation—marrying him—would cause her as much if not more pain and misery.

"Dixie and I need time to feel our way through the situation."

"Time is running out, Tucker. In another month she'll sport a baby bump."

The words *baby bump* echoed through Gavin's mind and his skin broke out in a cold sweat. "Dixie wants to focus on selling her soaps."

"That's another reason she needs to marry." Johnny shook his head. "She's got all these crazy business ideas running through her head. She needs a man to keep her in line."

Gavin smothered a smile behind a cough. Johnny didn't know his baby sister well if he believed Dixie would toe the line for Gavin, or any man for that matter.

"She thinks marketing her soaps on the internet will make her rich."

Gavin doubted the online business would earn enough money to improve Dixie's standard of living. That she'd protested vehemently when he'd suggested she set aside her soap-making while she raised the baby hinted that there was more behind her desire to sell suds than money. Gavin's gaze zeroed in on the phone number he'd scribbled on the workbench. Dixie had drawn a red heart around the digits. A surge of protectiveness filled him.

"It takes money to run a business," Johnny said. "Where's Dixie going to find the extra cash when she's raising a kid by herself?"

"I intend to help support the baby."

"But you won't be available to babysit so Dixie can

make the soaps or fill online orders, will you?" Gavin didn't have a chance to defend himself before Johnny added, "You're not good enough to make a living at rodeo."

"So you've said."

"How do you intend to support yourself as well as a kid if you don't have a nine-to-five job?"

"I could ask you the same question," Gavin said.

"First of all, I don't have a kid on the way, and second, I don't need a job—even though I work as a seasonal cowboy for the Triple D Ranch. The income from leasing the pecan farm supports me and my siblings."

"What happens when all of you marry? Will pecans still pay the bills and take care of your wives and children?"

Johnny glared.

"I'm not ready to quit rodeoing." Rodeo was the only thing helping Gavin ease back into civilian life. The thought of giving up the sport cold turkey was enough to make him physically ill.

"What happens if you get injured and can't rodeo?"

"Then I'll find a civilian job." He hoped that didn't happen anytime soon but if it did, his experience with water conservation and reclamation projects should help him find employment with a city water district.

"You need to look for work now rather than later."

Refusing to be bullied, Gavin said, "You need to let your sister and me figure things out."

Johnny backed off. "If you hurt Dixie, you'll have me and my brothers to answer to."

Gavin wasn't afraid of a fight—he'd been through several hand-to-hand scuffles in boot camp and his tour in Afghanistan, but he didn't want the situation between him and Dixie's brothers to escalate to that level. "Consider me warned."

"Warned about what?" Dixie waltzed into the barn.

Without missing a beat, Johnny said, "Your cooking. What's for supper?"

"I don't know." Dixie crinkled her nose. "What are *you* making?"

"I can cook," Gavin interrupted the squabbling pair. "I make a mean chili."

"Yeah, right," Johnny said.

"Be happy to show you." Maybe he could win Johnny over with food.

"Okay. The meat freezer is in the dining room."

Gavin trailed Johnny from the barn, leaving Dixie with her mouth hanging open.

"THIS IS THE BEST CHILI I've ever tasted," Porter said. Grunts of agreement followed the pronouncement.

Dixie silently fumed. She sat at the picnic table in the shade and scowled at her brothers who wolfed down the famous chili recipe Gavin had once cooked for the soldiers in his unit. His attempt to win favor with her brothers appeared to be working. She sampled another spoonful of the spicy concoction and covered her mouth to prevent a moan of appreciation from escaping.

"What's in this stuff?" Conway asked.

"Ground beef, Italian sausage, peppers, tomatoes and secret spices."

"Did you write down the recipe, Dix?" Johnny slurped a heaping spoonful.

"If you like it so much, you can make Gavin's chili next time," Dixie said.

Merle slouched in his chair and rubbed his belly. "How'd you learn to cook like this, Tucker?"

"I was raised by a single mom and she taught me to cook and sew."

"You sew?" Dixie blurted.

Gavin grinned. "I can sew a button on a shirt and I iron my own clothes."

The cowboy was Martha Stewart in disguise.

"What happened to your dad?" Buck, always the last to join a conversation, spoke up.

"He didn't stick around after I was born."

"What made you choose the army?" Willie asked, bombarding Gavin with more questions.

"Couldn't make enough money at rodeo and didn't want to go to college, so the military seemed like a good option."

"What'd you do in the army?" Buck asked.

"Provided Afghan villagers with clean drinking water in an effort to win their trust."

"Did it work?" Merle asked.

"Not really." Gavin's emotionless expression caused a pang in Dixie's heart. War left soldiers with scars—some visible, most invisible. What kind of baggage did the conflict in Afghanistan leave Gavin with?

Porter pushed his bowl aside. "What's for dessert?"

"Nothing." Dixie stood. "Gavin and I need to run an errand in town. We'll be back later." She cut across the yard and hopped into Gavin's truck.

"I guess we have an errand to run." Gavin set his spoon aside.

"Mind if I...?" Porter nodded to the chili remaining in Gavin's bowl.

"Help yourself."

"What do you think you're doing?" Dixie asked as soon as Gavin slid behind the steering wheel and started the truck.

"What are you talking about?"

"Cozying up to my brothers with delicious food and—"

"You think my chili's delicious?" He drove out of the yard.

"Never mind the chili. If you believe befriending my brothers will make me change my mind about allowing you to—"

Gavin slammed his boot on the brake and they rocked to a stop. Without warning he leaned across the front seat and kissed Dixie.

She'd dreamed of the kisses they'd shared in the motel room, but none of her fantasies had done justice to the real thing. When he pulled away, she pressed her fingers to her tingling lips. "What did you do that for?"

"You were getting too riled and that's not good for the baby."

The baby. Gavin had kissed her because he worried about the baby—not because he was attracted to her and couldn't help himself.

"I am not riled. I'm simply telling you that no one bosses me around, including my brothers."

"Where are we going?" Gavin turned onto the county road leading into Stagecoach.

"The drive-through."

"You could have had more chili."

"I'm not hungry. I want a root beer."

Gavin's gaze dropped to her stomach. "Are you experiencing cravings already?"

"No." She sighed. "I needed to get away from my brothers."

"I guess having six of them can be overwhelming."

After they'd passed the second mile marker, she asked, "Were you lonely growing up an only child?"

"Sometimes."

"Did you have a best friend?" Dixie considered Shannon Douglas her best friend. They'd hung out together in high school but after graduation Shannon had spent most of her time traveling the circuit, seeking out women's rough stock events to compete in and Dixie didn't see her friend as often as she'd like to.

"Nathan Parker was my best friend. We rodeoed in high school." Gavin chuckled. "During our first competition Nate got his front tooth knocked out and I broke my wrist."

"But the injuries didn't stop you from climbing onto another bronc."

"Nope. We rode the circuit after we graduated and when we ran out of entry-fee money we went down to the recruiter's office. Ended up going through boot camp together and got assigned to the same unit in Afghanistan."

"Is Nate still in the army?" If she hadn't been staring at Gavin's hands she would have missed the way his knuckles whitened against the wheel. A sense of forbidding spread through her. "You don't have to answer that. I have a bad habit of being nosy."

"It's all right. I told your brothers about him. Nate was killed three months before I left the military."

"I'm sorry, Gavin." She wanted to learn more about his best friend but hated for Gavin to relive painful memories, so she kept her questions to herself.

They arrived at the drive-in and a teenager stopped at Gavin's window. "What can I get you?"

"A number five meal and two large root beers." Gavin glanced at Dixie. "You made me leave before I finished my supper."

"Be ready in a jiffy." The teenager dropped off

their order with the cook, then meandered over to a car crowded with teenagers and chatted.

"Do you want to sit in the truck or outside?" He nodded to a table in the shade.

"Outside."

Once they were situated at the table, Gavin spoke. "Nate was killed by a roadside bomb."

Gavin's baggage from the war. Dixie's heart ached for him.

"I've gone over and over that day in my head, but I can't figure out what I missed."

"What you *missed*? I don't understand."

"We were installing an in-ground water filtration system. The people in the village had never given us any trouble and acted as if they appreciated our efforts to provide them with clean drinking water."

Dixie closed her eyes and pictured a dusty, barren village in the middle of mountainous terrain.

"I must have overlooked a clue—a warning the villagers were plotting against us. Late one afternoon we packed up to return to base camp and Nate wanted to drive the first Humvee in line. It was his birthday so I let him. When Nate walked up to the front of the vehicle, he stepped on a trip wire and set off the explosion."

Grasping Gavin's hand, Dixie squeezed hard. Nate had been blown up and Gavin had witnessed the tragic event—there were no words of comfort for that kind of horror.

Fearing his emotions would spiral out of control if he allowed himself to recall the details of that fateful day, Gavin gazed into Dixie's teary eyes, soaking in the sympathy and comfort shining in the blue depths. Their color reminded him of the Arizona sky on a cloudless day and slowly the tightness in his chest eased.

Their order arrived and he dug into his burger, disgusted by how easily he'd opened up to Dixie. At least he'd stopped babbling before he'd shared the gory details of Nate's death.

"You haven't told anyone about the baby, have you?" Dixie asked.

"I spoke to my mother," he said. "She knows."

Dixie stiffened. "And…?"

"She supports whatever decision we make about our situation."

"There's no decision to make." Dixie slurped the last of her root beer through the straw. "I'm not forcing you to be involved in the baby's life. You can come and go as you please."

A part of Gavin wished Dixie expected more from him. He was used to soldiers relying on him to solve problems and lead the way, but he also knew the best thing for Dixie and the baby was for him to keep his distance.

"How come you haven't told your brothers I'm the father?" he asked.

"Because they'd force you to marry me."

If Dixie discovered Johnny had already guessed on his own and had begun a marriage campaign on her behalf, she'd throw a fit.

"Marriage isn't an option." She made "I do" sound akin to torture.

He thought of his mother raising him alone and working two jobs to keep a roof over their heads. Sure, his situation with Dixie was different because he intended to pay child support, but what if Dixie carried a boy? There were times during his childhood when he'd yearned for a father to throw the baseball with or to coach his little league team. A father to help him buy his first car. To give him advice on girls. He'd missed not having a male role model in his life.

The sad truth was that no matter how Gavin might want to be involved in his child's life he didn't dare become a permanent fixture. But he'd show his son or daughter that he cared by making sure their mother didn't have to struggle financially, and he'd do his best to visit his child a few times a year.

Again Gavin's thoughts turned to his mother. Dixie hadn't been the only one who'd been teased because her father hadn't married her mother. Sylvia Tucker had also been a victim of gossip—neighbors, teachers and others in the community talking behind the single mother's back.

Marriage appeared to be the only way Gavin could protect Dixie and their child from vicious, hurtful ridicule.

"I've changed my mind," he said. "We're getting married."

"That sounds like a military order not a proposal." Dixie grimaced. "Why the sudden change of heart?"

Gavin couldn't ignore his deep sense of honor, but he also feared in doing the right thing he'd be the one making all the sacrifices. "You shouldn't have to raise our child alone." In reality, though, she would raise the baby without his help because he intended to remain a safe distance from them most of the time.

"Thanks, but no thanks." Dixie stood so fast she toppled her empty root beer mug. "I have my own plans and I won't allow you or anyone else to derail them."

"How would marrying me upset your plans?" To Gavin's way of thinking, he and Dixie would go their separate ways and come together on occasion for the baby's sake—birthdays and holidays.

She opened her mouth then snapped it shut. Rubbed her brow. Shook her head. Waved a hand in the air. She looked darn cute all fired up.

"Do you find the idea of marrying me repulsive?"

"Ha-ha." Her gaze zeroed in on Gavin's mouth, raising his body temperature several degrees. "You know you ooze sex appeal."

The disgusted tone in her voice equated *oozing sex appeal* to a draining-pustule disease.

"How long do you guess a marriage between us would last? A month? Just until the baby was born? Maybe a year afterward?" Dixie asked.

"Don't sound so optimistic."

"I'm serious. You and I know that you'd never have given me the time of day if Veronica hadn't been stalking you at the Boot Hill Rodeo."

That wasn't necessarily true but he doubted arguing the point would change Dixie's view. He studied the stubborn tilt of her chin. This was one fight Gavin would not win. He changed tactics. "What if we get engaged but hold off on a wedding until we know each other better." If Dixie still didn't want to marry then Gavin could walk away believing he'd done his duty.

"I have better things to do than spend time getting to know a man."

If Gavin wasn't able to support her and their child emotionally, he'd do it financially. "I'll invest in your soap company."

"Oh, no. I don't mind you offering me a loan like you already agreed to but I don't want you having a stake in my business."

"Why not?"

"Because, then you'd have a say in how I manage things."

"I don't want to tell you what to do with your soaps, Dixie." Investing in her company would be investing in his child's future.

"You'd give me money and not tell me what to do with it?"

"Consider me a silent partner." Dixie would find out soon enough how good he was at keeping things bottled up inside him.

"If I don't accept your engagement proposal will you rescind your previous offer to loan me a thousand dollars?"

He hadn't been thinking along those lines but since Dixie jumped to that conclusion he went with it. "We get engaged and you get the thousand dollars and access to more money if you need it." He crossed his arms over his chest and waited, confident she'd cave in.

Finally, her shoulders sagged. "I'll agree to the engagement as long as you understand it doesn't mean I'm agreeing to marriage."

"Deal." Her sassy demeanor amused Gavin. Beneath all that stubbornness was a sweet soul he found more and more difficult to resist. "Shall we seal our pact with a kiss?"

She slapped her open hand against his chest. "Whoa, soldier. Just because I agreed to a trial engagement doesn't mean you can have your way with me."

"It's a simple kiss, Dixie." He didn't give her time to reject him. He swooped in, pressing his mouth to hers, deepening the embrace—because she let him. Because she tasted of hope and goodness. Eventually the need for oxygen forced him to end the kiss.

"Gavin?"

"What?"

"Let me break the news to my brothers about our engagement."

That was one duty Gavin was willing to pass off to Dixie.

Chapter Six

"Where's Gavin?" Johnny's question greeted Dixie when she entered the farmhouse kitchen. Her eldest brother sat alone at the table, nursing a beer.

"He left." As soon as they'd returned from town. Dixie assumed Gavin hadn't wanted to stay for fear she'd change her mind about their engagement.

"Did you ask him where he was headed?"

It was bad enough that her pregnancy caused occasional bouts of morning sickness, excessive sleepiness and numerous trips to the bathroom in the middle of the night—she had little energy left to contend with bossy brothers. "What Gavin does is none of my business." And he had no say in what she did.

Johnny leaned across the kitchen table. "Tucker's whereabouts sure in heck oughtta be your business, little sister."

Dixie had had enough of well-meaning men for one day. She planted her fists on her hips and ignored the squeaking sounds of the bedroom doors in the upstairs hallway. "Gavin has his life and I have mine."

"The hell you say!" Johnny's fist slammed against the table. "He's the father of your baby."

Although Dixie hadn't come right out and said Gavin was the father, she believed Johnny had guessed the first time Gavin visited the farm. "So what if he is the father?" The heat and the fact that she had a craving for chocolate when there were no sweets in the house made her irritable.

"You and Tucker are getting married pronto."

"Oh, really? Do you plan to drag me to the church by my hair?"

Voices whispered in the upstairs hallway—no doubt her brothers were holding a family conference, debating how best to defend her honor.

"After what Mom put us through, how can you consider raising your baby out of wedlock?"

Johnny had gone for the jugular. He, more than the others, understood how difficult it had been for her to be the only daughter of a promiscuous mother. "Don't get your tighty-whities twisted in a knot. Gavin proposed this afternoon."

She neglected to tell Johnny that the engagement was a sham and she had no intention of marrying Gavin. Once word spread that she and Gavin were engaged and she was expecting his baby, they'd become old news and people would move on to greener gossip pastures. She'd wait a month or two after the baby was born then end their engagement and raise the child alone—as she'd planned to do all along.

"About time you came to your senses."

Dixie opened her mouth to argue but yawned instead.

"You're tired."

"I hate it when you do that," she said.

"Do what?"

"Tell me what I'm feeling."

Johnny raised an eyebrow. "You need a nap."

Swallowing a sarcastic retort, Dixie left the kitchen, her brother stalking her through the hallway.

"When's the wedding?" he asked.

"We haven't settled on a date."

"Why not?"

Her brothers had gathered on the landing, their gazes shifting between Dixie and their big brother.

"I'm going to take a nap." She climbed the stairs and shoved her way through the human barricade. "Leave me alone." She punctuated the command with the slamming of her bedroom door at the end of the hall.

After Dixie's birth, her grandfather had expanded the linen closet into the attic, turning the space into a nursery. The room's slanted ceiling made it impossible for her brothers to stand up straight without hitting their heads, so they rarely ventured inside the room. A window air conditioner kept the cramped quarters cool. She stretched out on the twin bed and stared at the ceiling. Her throat grew thick. Her eyes burned and chest ached.

I will not cry. The silent declaration opened the floodgates and tears leaked from her eyes.

Dixie's heart had stopped beating when Gavin had insisted they marry, and for an instant, she'd believed he'd wanted to make him, her and the baby a real family.

Stupid. Stupid. Stupid.

She lifted the corner of the sheet and dabbed her tears. Her reaction had been childish. It had only been a matter of time before Gavin insisted on marriage—for the baby's sake, not hers. She cursed herself for agreeing to a trial engagement, realizing now that she'd set herself up for more heartache and—

"Mind if I come in?"

"I'm napping, Porter."

As if the statement had been an invitation, Porter ducked inside. Shoulders hunched, he crossed the room and sat at the foot of her bed.

"Johnny said you and Gavin are engaged."

She flipped onto her side, facing the wall.

"Aren't you happy the father of your baby's going to do right by you?"

"Gavin doesn't need to marry me to send child-support checks."

"You don't want to marry him?" Porter stood and knocked his head on the ceiling. "Ouch."

"I don't love Gavin." As soon as she said the words, a voice inside her head mocked her with laughter. Dixie rolled away from the wall. "Would you marry a girl you got pregnant if you didn't love her?"

Porter's cheeks turned red. "I guess, if I had to."

Dixie rolled her eyes.

"Gavin seems like a nice guy. He fits in with the rest of us and he can cook a mean pot of chili. You could do worse than him for a husband."

"Gavin's a saint, that's for sure."

"Johnny thinks you're going to sabotage your engagement."

Darn her older brother for seeing through her. "Exactly how would I do that?"

Porter shrugged. "Johnny says you should quit selling your soap and focus on Gavin and the baby."

She refused to put aside her goals and desires for the baby. Other women had careers while raising children—she could do it, too. "Get out."

Her brother hunch-walked to the door. "Did Gavin give you an engagement ring?"

Since she had no intention of dragging out their engagement charade longer than necessary, she didn't expect Gavin to waste his money on a diamond. Still…a ring would quiet the gossipmongers. "Leave me alone."

Shaking his head Porter left her in peace. Murmurs

from the hallway drifted beneath the door but Dixie ignored them and placed a hand over her tummy. She concentrated on the baby growing inside her; her final thought before drifting off to sleep was whether or not the baby would have Gavin's brown eyes.

GAVIN TIGHTENED HIS leather riding glove then flexed his fingers. Almost two weeks had passed since he'd proposed to Dixie and they'd spoken only a few times on the phone. Aside from polite, meaningless conversation, she never brought up the baby and neither did Gavin.

He'd had plenty of time to contemplate the future during the long, solitary drives between rodeos, but he'd yet to come to terms with his impending fatherhood. That didn't bother him as much as the realization that when he was apart from Dixie he missed her.

The few times they'd spoken, he'd asked when the marketing firm would have her website up and running, but Dixie hadn't given a clear answer and had changed the subject. Maybe she believed his interest in her business was self-serving since he'd loaned her money. He should be grateful she kept him at arm's length, but he found her coolness irritating.

If anything good had come from proposing to Dixie it was that the Cash brothers had quit following him on the circuit. If only he could find his seat again and make it to eight on a bronc, he'd feel better about the future. His confidence faltering, Gavin worried that the rodeo career he'd mapped out for himself was nothing more than a pipe dream. The only consolation after each loss was that when he closed his eyes at night and saw Nate's mutilated body, he focused on Dixie and eventually the blood and gore gave way to sleep.

Dixie was an enigma—stubborn, bossy and opinionated. Yet, when he'd held her in his arms and had made love to her she'd been soft, sweet and achingly vulnerable. He clung to the memory of her sexy sighs and gentle caresses, which carried him to a peaceful place each night.

"Fans, Gavin Tucker's up next in the bareback riding competition!" the rodeo announcer said.

Pushing Dixie to the far reaches of his mind, Gavin climbed the chute rails and straddled Twinkle. He'd picked the Blythe Rodeo on a whim, hoping the added practice would prepare him for the next go-round in Bullhead City the following weekend where the pot was ten grand.

"Tucker's drawn Twinkle." The announcer chuckled. "Twinkle's got the personality of a rattler. Cowboys never know when this bronc's gonna toss 'em on their head."

Gavin had heard his competitors gossiping about the horse earlier in the day. The bronc was an arm jerker— a stout horse that bucked with a lot of power. If a cowboy managed to keep his seat on Twinkle, he'd earn big points. Gavin tested his grip, then took a deep breath and nodded to the gateman.

Twinkle leaped for freedom and it took all of Gavin's strength to hold on. He leaned back and spurred the gelding. So far so good. Twinkle switched direction every other buck, forcing Gavin's thigh muscles to work overtime as he fought to keep his balance. Sweat ran into his eyes but he ignored the sting, as he gauged the bronc's next move. Right before the buzzer sounded, Gavin's arm gave out and Twinkle sent him sailing through the air. He landed face-first on the ground and swallowed a mouthful of dirt.

As Twinkle trotted from the arena, Gavin slowly got

to his feet. The first few steps were the toughest—testing his muscles, evaluating injuries. Today he'd gotten off easy—a few aches, pains and twinges.

"Looks as if Twinkle outsmarted Tucker. Better luck next time, cowboy!"

Gavin waved his hat to the crowd, then hobbled into the cowboy ready area where he collected his gear. He'd grab a hotdog from the concession stand and hit the road.

"Long time no see, soldier."

Gavin's stomach clenched at the sound of the silky voice. He turned and came face-to-face with Veronica. He'd thought he'd seen the last of her a month ago.

"Are the rumors true?"

He played dumb. "What rumors?"

"The ones sayin' you're engaged."

"Who'd you hear that from?"

"Porter Cash. He's been telling everyone he runs into that you're marrying his sister."

Gavin didn't blame the Cash brothers for wanting folks to know Dixie was engaged before news of her pregnancy spread. "It's true. We're engaged."

The corner of Veronica's mouth curled. "You knocked her up, didn't you?"

He'd never believed in his wildest imagination that he'd get a girl pregnant by accident but thank God the girl had been Dixie and not Veronica. Gavin hoisted his gear bag onto his shoulder. "Enjoy the rest of the rodeo."

Long, red talons sank into his forearm when he attempted to pass Veronica. "If things don't work out with Dixie…"

He yanked his arm free and moseyed off.

"Dixie can't handle a man like you," she called after him.

Gavin kept walking and ignored the looks of his competitors. Forgetting about his hotdog he left the arena and zigzagged through the parking lot to his truck. While he waited for the air conditioner to cool off the interior, he checked his phone for messages. None. He shifted the truck into Drive and sped away.

Another rodeo. Another loss. Another solitary night on the road.

Except for the losing part—exactly what he'd wanted when he'd quit the army. He should feel fortunate that the woman carrying his baby had no plans to interfere with his nomadic life, instead, he resented Dixie's standoffish attitude.

Maybe she senses a darkness inside you.

Was it possible that Dixie might be leery of getting closer to Gavin? The only way to find out was to ask Dixie if she was afraid of him and Gavin sure in heck wasn't opening that can of worms.

The next time he paid attention to the highway signs he discovered he'd missed his turnoff and was driving south. Like a homing pigeon his instinct was to return to Dixie. He had five days until his next ride. He might as well blow them on the Cash pecan farm.

Gavin flipped on the turn signal and took the exit for Stagecoach. With each passing mile, his heart beat faster. His and Dixie's one-night stand had been a fluke, yet there was no denying they'd hit it off in bed. He wanted to make love to her again but feared the closeness would weaken his resolve to keep his distance from her and the baby.

Squirming against the snugness of his jeans, Gavin slowed the truck at the edge of town. He stopped at the only traffic light and tapped his fingers against the steering wheel. He should bring Dixie a present. Glancing along the block of storefronts he studied his options.

Food. Liquor. A gift certificate from the Bee Luv Lee Hair Salon. Did the grocery mart at the gas station sell flowers? The light turned green and he drove another block before hitting the brakes in front of the Pawn Palace. He studied the gadgets in the store window, his gaze zeroing in on a sparkly object in the corner.

A diamond ring.

Crap. He'd been so focused on doing the right thing that he'd gone about it backward. He must have hurt Dixie's feelings when he'd proposed to her without an engagement ring. He put the truck in Park and went into the store. Fifteen minutes later and a hundred-fifty bucks poorer, Gavin drove out to the pecan farm.

He didn't expect a pawn-shop ring to win him any points, but when he pulled up to the house, Gavin was contemplating ways to steal a kiss from Dixie before the evening ended. Her pickup was the only vehicle in the yard. He'd forgotten about the truck breaking down and was relieved it had been repaired. In her condition Dixie shouldn't be without reliable transportation.

He parked by the barn, figuring Dixie would be in her workshop but all the lights were off. He did an about-face and returned to the house, knocking twice on the front door. No answer. He peered through the window, but the foyer was empty. He tried the doorknob—unlocked. "Dixie!" he shouted when he stepped inside.

He checked the kitchen. Empty. Where was she? He left through the back door and hiked into the pecan grove. Maybe she was gathering herbs or flowers or whatever she used to make organic soap. He'd walked a quarter mile when his ears perked. He stopped and listened to a hollow thudlike sound, then switched directions, cutting through a row of trees before pulling up short.

Dixie stood ten yards away, throwing stones at the trunk of an ancient pecan tree. A pile of rocks rested at her feet. Throw after throw the rocks whittled a divot in the bark. If Dixie's soap business tanked she could try out for a major league baseball team—the girl's aim was dead-on.

"Strike three, he's out!" Gavin shouted.

Dixie spun, stumbling off balance. Gavin rushed forward, offering a steady hand.

"Sorry. I didn't mean to frighten you."

"What are you doing here?" She swiped angrily at the tears staining her cheeks.

"You're crying."

"I'm sweating." *Darn.* The cowboy popped in and out of Dixie's life at the most inconvenient times.

"I was passing through the area and thought I'd see how you're doing."

"Just because we're engaged doesn't give you the right to check up on me."

He raised his hands in the air. "Are you upset because I've been on the road?"

"Don't get a big head." She scrunched her nose. "You're not the reason I'm crying."

"You said you were sweating."

She sniffed, then kicked the pile of rocks she'd spent an hour gathering.

Gavin inched closer and tucked a strand of hair behind her ear. His fingers lingered against her skin and she shivered at the intimate touch. "Tell me why you're upset. I want to help," he said.

It took more effort than expected to rein in her emotions. She'd had herself a good cry, now she had to decide on the next course of action. "You can't fix this."

"Try me."

Dixie was no match for Gavin's sympathetic gaze. "Today I learned that the marketing firm I paid five thousand dollars to design my business website turned out to be a bogus company." Lord, she couldn't believe how gullible she'd been. She braced herself, expecting Gavin to implode. He didn't.

"What do you mean 'bogus company'?"

"My design agent disappeared off the face of the earth. His 800 number's been disconnected and the internet address for the company's website no longer exists."

"Have you reported this to anyone?"

"I contacted the Internet Crime Complaint Center and filed a report."

"Did you call your bank to put a hold on the check?"

"Yes, but the creep had already cashed it." Through veiled eyes she studied Gavin.

Her brothers, who were technically challenged except when it came to playing video games on their Xbox had warned her not to do business with an internet company. But Dixie had done her homework—or so she'd believed. The scam artist had posted bogus reviews for his company and must have had friends involved in the con, because the woman she'd emailed asking questions about her experience with the marketing firm had given Dixie all the right answers and a link to her newly designed website, which Dixie discovered had also disappeared from the internet. "Go ahead and say it."

"Say what?"

"I told you so." Gavin remained silent. "I'll pay back the money you loaned me." Who knew how long it would take to save up a thousand dollars? The tears that were never far from the surface these days dribbled down her cheeks and she batted away the wetness. "All I ever wanted was to make my grandmother's dream come true."

Gavin took her hand and led her to the tree she'd used for target practice. They sat on the ground and leaned their backs against the trunk. He didn't pressure her to talk and after a few minutes she relaxed. She wasn't used to sharing her fears or dreams—blame it on pregnancy hormones, but Dixie needed to vent.

"My grandmother was more of a mother to me than my own mom," she said. While Aimee Cash had chased after men, Grandma Ada had spent time teaching Dixie to keep house, cook and make the family soap recipes, which dated back six generations in France.

"Grandma Ada dreamed of selling her soaps to a big company like Colgate, but my grandfather told her that she was foolish if she believed they'd take notice of her homemade soaps."

Gavin wiped the tears marring Dixie's cheeks. Her long, brown lashes swept down, concealing her blue eyes. The need to hug her was powerful, but he hesitated. Along with wanting to comfort Dixie came a strong urge to help fulfill her dream.

He blamed his years in the army for his need to step in and take over. He was a problem solver. A fix-it man. But it was more than instinct that prompted him to lead—he genuinely cared about Dixie. "I'll loan you the money to work with another marketing firm."

"Thanks, but no, thanks. I'm finished doing business online."

Time passed and neither spoke, and then Dixie's head bumped Gavin's shoulder and he realized she'd dozed off. The weight of her resting against him felt right. Comfortable.

Now that he understood Dixie's passion for soap-making was tied to her love for her grandmother he was determined to do everything possible to help her succeed. The sun drifted lower in the sky, casting shadows across the trees and darkening the grove. He wasn't sure how long they sat when the rumble of pickups reached his ears.

Gavin gently nudged Dixie's shoulder but she burrowed deeper against his side. Taking advantage of her sleepiness he lifted her chin and pressed his mouth to hers. Her lashes flew up and he waited for her to object—instead she curled her arms around his neck and opened her mouth wider. The tip of her tongue touched his lips and his arousal shot off the charts. He drowned in Dixie—her soft breasts rubbing against his chest, the taste of her sweet mouth, the scent of her honeysuckle shampoo. He pressed his erection against her thigh and groaned.

Dixie popped open the snaps on his shirt. When her cool fingers stroked his naked chest, Gavin lost what little control he had. He pulled the hem of her shirt from her jeans and slipped his hand beneath the cotton. Sliding his fingers across her warm skin, he cupped her breast and thumbed her pert nipple through the silky fabric of her bra.

The sound of a throat clearing brought Gavin back to his senses and he pulled away from Dixie. The Cash brothers had crashed his party. Johnny, Merle and Buck scowled. Porter grinned. Willie and Conway appeared indifferent to catching their sister lip-locked with Gavin.

Dixie continued kissing him. "We've got company," Gavin mumbled against her mouth.

She sucked in a quiet breath, then scrambled to her feet and attempted to straighten her shirt and smooth her mussed hair.

When Johnny's gaze zeroed in on the front of Gavin's unsnapped shirt, Gavin quickly fixed the problem. Shoot, it wasn't as if he and Dixie had been caught frolicking beneath the pecan tree buck naked.

"Dixie—"

"Don't say a word." Brushing the dust off her fanny, she marched past her brothers, leaving Gavin alone to face the firing squad.

"Until my sister's wearing an engagement ring, you keep your hands to yourself, Tucker," Johnny warned. The remaining Cash brothers nodded in agreement and followed their sister back to the farmhouse.

Gavin stuffed his hand in his jean pocket and touched the pawnshop ring box. Now was probably a good time to officially propose. When he got back to the house Dixie's brothers were lounging on the porch. He stopped at the bottom step. "Dixie!"

The screen door squeaked open and she stepped outside.

Gavin had hoped for a more private place to present Dixie with the ring. He climbed the steps and took her left hand in his, then slipped the silver band with diamond chips onto her finger.

Dixie frowned. "What's this?"

"An engagement ring."

The Cash brothers gathered close and examined the piece of jewelry. They twisted Dixie's hand one way then the other, lifting it toward the light. "I can't tell," Merle said. "Are those diamonds or cut glass?"

"I'll buy you a bigger diamond, if you want," Gavin said.

"Don't bother." Dixie retreated inside.

"Way to go, Romeo." Conway spat tobacco juice into the bushes, then the brothers filed into the house, leaving Gavin alone outside.

Well, hell. He'd done what Johnny had asked, hadn't he? Gavin descended the steps and walked to his truck. After the heated kiss he and Dixie had shared, they needed time to cool off—who knows how far things would have gone between them if her brothers hadn't interrupted. At least nothing had happened—this time.

If Gavin knew what was good for himself he'd make sure there was no next time.

Chapter Seven

"Oh, for goodness' sake, spit it out," Dixie said. Her brothers sat at the dining-room table playing with their fries and chicken wings, while casting puzzled glances her way. She supposed they questioned why she hadn't invited Gavin for supper after he'd given her the engagement ring.

Johnny pushed his plate aside, then nodded to the band on Dixie's finger. "You haven't set a wedding date."

"So?"

"You'll be showing soon and people will wonder when you and Gavin are tying the knot," Johnny said.

"Let them wonder."

"It's not a big deal, Dixie. Pick a damn date and we'll speak to Reverend Thomas about—"

"I'll get married when—" *and if* "—I want to." Dixie ignored her brothers' gapes and continued eating. If she told the truth—that she'd hoodwinked Gavin into agreeing to an engagement on a trial-run basis, allowing him to believe she'd succumb in the end and marry him when in reality she had no intention of doing so—her brothers would carry her bound and gagged to the altar.

Buck's quiet yet firm voice broke the silence in the room. "You're wearing Gavin's ring."

Dixie's eyes stung at the reminder. That Gavin had bought her an engagement ring as an afterthought shouldn't hurt, but it did.

"A ring means you intend to marry." Johnny scowled.

"I'm twenty-three years old. Stop telling me what to do." She tossed her napkin on the table. "I'll be in the barn."

Dixie had more to worry about than booking a Saturday wedding at the local chapel. She still hadn't told her brothers she'd been scammed out of five thousand dollars by a bogus online marketing firm. Inside the barn she switched on the lights and surveyed the messy worktable covered in spools of decorative ribbon and sheets of colored tissue paper. The tears she'd struggled to hold back during supper dribbled down her cheeks. Darn her seesawing hormones.

What to do... Although Dixie appreciated Gavin offering her additional money to hire a new marketing company, she'd lost her entrepreneurial courage and self-doubt had gained a foothold inside her. She'd been a naive fool to believe she could bring her grandmother's dream to life.

Forcing the morose thoughts aside, she organized her supplies and stowed the herbs in airtight containers. She lost track of the time and not until headlights swept across the barn doors did she realize the sun had set. Thinking Gavin had returned, Dixie smoothed her hair and straightened her shirt before stepping from the barn and spotting Shannon Douglas's white extended-cab pickup. Hiding her disappointment she pasted a smile on her face.

"Hey, Shannon." Dixie's smile faltered when her friend's expression remained sober. "Congrats on being sponsored by Wrangler." Johnny had told Dixie the news.

"Thanks." Shannon's green eyes dropped to Dixie's stomach. "How are you feeling?"

"Fine. Why?"

Shannon stepped past Dixie and examined the soap molds. "I haven't heard from you in forever."

Shannon and Dixie used to talk once a week, a simple how's-it-going call. They'd chat about Shannon's latest ride, or a cute cowboy one of them had run into.

"I was afraid you were still mad at me for bailing on you at the Piney Gorge Rodeo."

"I'm not mad, Dix." Shannon frowned. "Why are you here at the farm while Gavin's riding the circuit?"

"Where else would I be?"

"With him."

"It's not like that between us." Dixie rubbed her thumb over Gavin's phone number inside the heart she'd drawn. "We're not jumping into marriage but he is going to support the baby."

"You're wearing an engagement ring." Shannon's gaze shifted to Dixie's hand.

"Gavin doesn't want people to think bad of me."

"Are you dragging your feet, because Gavin doesn't seem like the kind of guy to dodge responsibility?"

There was that damned word again—*responsibility*. "I've got six brothers who are fit to be tied over me getting pregnant. I don't need my best friend upset with me, too."

"I'm not upset," Shannon insisted. "But I know what you went through when people ridiculed your mother."

"Times have changed."

"People haven't, Dixie. Maybe you don't care what folks say about you but think of the baby."

"Gavin and I plan to remain engaged until the baby's born."

"Then what—Gavin's off the hook?"

No, I'm off the hook. Dixie felt guilty that Gavin appeared the bad guy when in truth she was the villain. "Gavin's not walking away from his responsibilities. He's committed to his child."

Shannon opened her mouth, then shook her head and changed the subject. "I dropped by to invite you to the Bullhead City Rodeo next Saturday. If I win, Wrangler will fly me to Florida to compete in a special women's rough stock event which will be broadcast live on TV."

"I'd love to watch you ride," Dixie said.

"Bullhead City is four hours away. You shouldn't make the drive alone in case—"

"I'm pregnant, not dying from an incurable disease."

Shannon laughed. "I can't picture you a mother."

"Thanks."

"I hope it's a boy."

"Why?"

"Because you're a tomboy and you wouldn't know the first thing about playing with dolls or having tea parties."

"You can leave now if you're through badgering me."

"Yeah, yeah, I'm going." Shannon hugged Dixie. "Take care of yourself."

"I will. And, Shannon…thanks for stopping by."

"No problem. I want to make sure that kid knows I'm his favorite aunt."

Dixie watched the taillights of Shannon's truck disappear. Resting a hand over her tummy, she asked, "Are you a boy or a girl?" At only ten weeks pregnant Dixie hadn't felt the baby kick. The doctor told her to expect a fluttering sensation between the sixteenth and eighteenth week—the time Dixie had hoped to launch her website business. She'd so wanted a game plan in place for supporting her child before she felt the first kick and the baby suddenly became *real*.

She closed her eyes and thought back to earlier in the afternoon when Gavin had kissed her in the pecan grove. He was an accomplished kisser—just the right amount of pressure, tongue, nibbles and nuzzles to make her crave more.

After discovering she'd been ripped off by the phony marketing firm she'd channeled her fear into anger. When Gavin had caught her throwing rocks at the tree, the anger had given way to fear again. The impulse to rush into his arms and trust him to right the wrongs done to her had scared Dixie to death. Her grandmother had taught her to be self-sufficient and relying on Gavin would only hurt her in the long run. When the wander-lust bug bit him, he'd return to rodeo and leave Dixie with a broken heart.

Dixie was certain she'd pegged Gavin correctly—so why had he bothered with an engagement ring? She twirled the band on her finger. As far as rings went this one was old-fashioned—certainly nothing that spoke of a man's undying love and passion for his bride-to-be.

Was there a chance Gavin might one day possess real feelings for her—not thoughts of responsibility toward her and the baby, but genuine, heartfelt caring? Did she dare believe she and Gavin could make it as a couple?

No. The only reason Gavin remained a part of her life was because of the baby. To believe anything more would bring heartbreak—hers.

Her gaze returned to Gavin's cell number. She was capable of driving four hours to a rodeo and back home the same day. Besides, one or more of her brothers was

probably headed to the same rodeo. A four-hour inqui-
sition from her brothers was enough to convince her to
call Gavin. She pushed two on her speed dial.

"What's wrong, Dixie?"

Gavin's abrupt question startled her, leaving her
speechless.

"Dixie? You there?"

"I'm here and nothing's the matter."

"You never call. I thought…"

"Got a minute?"

"Sure."

Instead of discussing the upcoming Bullhead City
Rodeo, she said, "You didn't stay for supper."

"I wasn't invited."

"In case you weren't aware," she said, "my brothers
and I haven't had the privilege of attending Miss Manners Charm School."

"Are you being funny, Ms. Cash?"

Dixie smiled at the note of humor in Gavin's voice.
"Hardly."

"What's on your mind?"

"Do you plan to ride in the Bullhead City Rodeo
next Saturday?"

"I had planned to. Why?"

"Shannon Douglas wants me to watch her compete
and I thought maybe I could hitch a ride with you."

"I'll pick you up early in the morning."

Silence filled the connection, then they spoke si-
multaneously.

"Gavin."

"Dixie."

"You go first," he said.

"No, you."

"Never mind, it was nothing. See you Saturday," he said.

"Okay, sure."

"And, Dixie?"

"What?"

"I'm sorry about the jerk who stole your money."

Dixie's throat swelled with emotion. "Good night." Gavin was far from perfect but he was a decent, caring—*sexy*—man.

You keep forgetting you're not his type.

Baby aside, if Gavin had his pick of women, no way would he choose a pecan farmer's granddaughter. Dixie would just have to settle for Gavin coming in and out of her life to visit the baby. Now, if only he'd cooperate and stop making her want him.

Wow.

Gavin's eyes were glued to Dixie who stood on the porch waiting for him as he barreled up the drive. She looked *h-o-t* in the denim miniskirt and bandanna-print tank top. Red boots drew his attention to her sexy legs. No man on earth would look at this woman and suspect she was pregnant.

Gavin shifted into Park and frowned. Why was Dixie dressed to kill? They were going to a rodeo, not a night on the town and besides, she *was* pregnant *and* engaged.

Maybe she dressed that way for you.

Yeah, right. Dixie's lack of excitement when he'd slid the engagement ring on her finger was proof enough she had reservations about him. *What did you expect?*

Okay, so his official proposal wasn't exactly a romantic bended-knee declaration of undying love, but she could cut him some slack—her brothers had been watching.

You gave her someone's cast-off ring.

Gavin hopped out of the truck and rounded the hood, opening the passenger-side door and offering Dixie a hand up. *She painted her nails.* The bright red color was at odds with the down-to-earth woman he knew.

"Thanks for letting me tag along to the rodeo." She tugged her hand free and shut the door in his face.

They hadn't seen each other in six days—didn't that at least merit a smile?

The past week had been a whirlwind of activity as he'd come to accept that if he pushed Dixie too hard about marriage she'd flee across the border to Mexico to escape exchanging vows with him. In any event, he decided that if he got to pursue his own itinerary Dixie should be allowed to do the same.

When he got in the truck, the scent of honeysuckle surrounded him—better than the usual fast-food and coffee smells. "You look nice," he said, starting the engine.

"Thanks."

"Are your brothers competing today?"

"I think Merle and Buck are. They left at the crack of dawn."

They drove in silence to the main road. "When's your next doctor's appointment?"

"I had one yesterday."

He waited for Dixie to tell him how she and the baby were doing but she didn't. "Everything okay with—"

"The baby's fine."

"What about you?"

"What about me?"

She had to know he was concerned about her health, too. "Did the doctor say you're fine, as well?"

"Yes."

Communicating with an Afghan villager was easier than conversing with Dixie. Maybe she wasn't comfortable discussing the changes in her body. He pushed her. "Do you have morning sickness?"

"I did, but this past week it tapered off."

"What about cravings?"

"Pickles."

He chuckled. "No sweet cravings like ice cream or pie?" Gavin's mother had told him that she'd loved banana splits while she'd been pregnant with him.

"Not yet, thank goodness. I'm hoping I don't gain too much weight with this pregnancy."

"You won't have a problem losing whatever you gain." He cast an appreciative glance across the seat. "You're in great shape." His compliment turned her cheeks pink.

"What have you been up to lately?" she asked.

Aside from seeing Dixie's dream come to fruition... "I competed in a small rodeo up in Blythe this past Sunday. A one-day event."

"How'd you—"

"Lost." *Again.*

"Did you run into Veronica Patriot there?"

"Yep." That Dixie worried about the buckle bunny convinced Gavin she wasn't as immune to him as she'd have him believe. "Veronica wanted to know if the rumors were true." He looked at Dixie. "If we were engaged."

"What did you tell her?"

"The truth."

"She must have freaked out."

"She wasn't happy."

Dixie drummed her fingers on the armrest. "Mind if I ask a personal question?"

"Go right ahead."

"When you're not rodeoing…where's home?"

If he said his truck would she think him pathetic? "My mother's place in Phoenix." A partial truth. On occasion he visited his mother but never stayed the night. Mostly he lived in motel rooms or slept in the backseat of his truck.

He turned on the radio, exhaling a shaky breath when Dixie reclined in her seat and closed her eyes. He'd keep quiet so she could catch a nap before they arrived in Bullhead City. He wanted her in a good mood later tonight when he stopped in Yuma to show her the surprise he'd put together this week for her.

Delayed by construction on Highway 95, Gavin didn't pull up to the fairgrounds until almost noon. When he didn't grab his gear from the backseat Dixie frowned. "I thought you were riding today?"

"Changed my mind," he said. No way would he have been able to concentrate, knowing Dixie was in the stands watching him. They weaved their way through the crowd inside the arena.

"What made you change your mind?" she asked.

"I tweaked my shoulder during the last rodeo and it's still sore," he fibbed.

"Maybe you should see a doctor."

The concern in Dixie's voice surprised Gavin. He couldn't remember anyone, save for his mother, worrying about him. "I'll get to a doctor if it's not better in a week."

"Probably a pinched nerve. Conway suffered one in his neck last year and was a bear to live with until the pain went away."

Thanks to the army the words *suck it up* had been drilled into Gavin's brain and he rarely complained.

What would it be like to come home at the end of the day to a woman who listened to his grumbles and offered a sympathetic hug? Gavin guided Dixie past a group of chattering teens.

"Here we are." He led Dixie through the row until they located their seat numbers. "Are you hungry?" he asked.

"Not really."

"How about a drink?"

"A water would be nice," she said.

"Comin' right up." Gavin headed for the concession stand, but halfway there Veronica Patriot stepped into his path.

"Hello, Gavin." Her gaze traveled over his body, her eyes widening when she saw his dress boots. "You're not competing today?"

"Nope." He attempted to move past her but Veronica slid sideways and he bumped into her triple D's.

"Why in such a hurry?" Her mouth curved in invitation.

Frustrated, Gavin swallowed a cuss word. "I'm here with Dixie."

Veronica's mouth curled in a snarl. "Your fiancée?"

He considered telling the pesky tramp to go screw a fence post and leave him alone but instead walked off without a word.

As Gavin stood in the concession line, he reflected on the past few nights in which he'd drifted off to sleep with his thoughts on Dixie. He'd learned that as long as he focused on her, the nightmares that had haunted him since leaving Afghanistan lost their razor-sharp edges.

He'd gotten so caught up in his plans for Dixie this past week that he had to remind himself that what he'd done had been for the baby, too—not just for Dixie, although pleasing her made him feel good. And worthy.

Dixie affected Gavin in a way no one had since he'd left the army. He didn't understand the spell she'd cast over him, but he was beginning to believe that tying himself to one person for the rest of his life might not be as scary as he'd once thought.

Chapter Eight

"Ladies and gentlemen, welcome to Bullhead City's sixty-first annual Cowboy Festival and Rodeo." The JumboTron flashed still photos of the cowboys competing in the day's events. Dixie ignored the pomp and pageantry and wiggled in her bleacher seat. Gavin took up his space and part of hers, making it impossible to prevent their legs from touching. The heat radiating from his thigh was distracting and downright arousing.

"They wrote about Shannon." Gavin pointed to the article in the brochure he'd purchased from a program hawker.

"What does it say?" Using the write-up as an excuse to lean against Gavin's arm, Dixie closed her eyes and breathed in the clean masculine scent of his woodsy cologne.

"A spokesperson from Wrangler says… 'Shannon Douglas is the first female rodeo athlete to come along who has the skill, determination and stamina to compete with the men.'" Gavin straightened in his seat. "I hope she can back that statement with a winning ride."

"She will." Like Dixie, Shannon had grown up with brothers—no sisters. In order to survive the physical roughhousing and teasing among their siblings, they had both developed a mental and physical toughness.

"Folks, we have a special event this afternoon sponsored by Wrangler." The fans applauded. When the noise died down the announcer continued. "For those of you who aren't familiar with the name Shannon Douglas—" a chuckle followed "—you will be in a few minutes. Shannon and Wrangler have teamed up to promote women's rough stock events. We all know cowgirls are tough inside and out but only the toughest gals ride bulls."

Music and action photos of Shannon's summer rodeos flashed across the JumboTron. "Shannon Douglas is a native of Stagecoach, Arizona, and one of the few women in the United States who'll take on fifteen-hundred pounds of buckin' rage." The fans stomped their boots on the bleachers and Dixie winced at the ear-splitting din.

"Shannon's gonna kick off the men's bull ridin' event by showin' us she can compete with the best cowboys on the circuit. Turn your attention to gate number five. Looks like C. J. Rodriguez is placin' a bet with Shannon right now."

Dixie spotted Shannon seated on the bull in the chute and C.J. perched on the rails next to her. Money exchanged hands and the audience cheered.

"Hey, C.J.!" The announcer's shout echoed through the arena and C.J.'s head popped up. "You bettin' Shannon makes it to eight?"

C.J. shook his head *no* and the crowd roared, half booing C.J. the other half cheering him.

"C.J. that ain't very supportive," the announcer teased.

Shannon smacked C.J. in the chest with her hat and he held it while Shannon placed a protective helmet and mask over her head and face. Before she signaled the gateman, she and C.J. fist-bumped, and then the cowboy dropped out of sight and the chute door opened.

"Here comes Shannon Douglas on Boilermaker!"

Dixie clutched Gavin's rock-hard thigh and held her breath as she counted off the seconds. Boilermaker fell into a pattern of bucking twice then spinning. The bull flung, whipped and jerked Shannon's body every which way but the cowgirl hung on.

Six...seven...eight! Dixie popped out of her seat, stuck her fingers in her mouth and whistled for all she was worth. Amid the thunderous applause the bullfighters helped Shannon free her hand from the rope. As soon as she landed in the dirt she rolled to her feet then scampered toward the rails, Boilermaker hot on her heels.

The bull gained ground on Shannon and a collective gasp echoed through the arena. Boilermaker rammed his horns into the rails inches from Shannon's boots, but C. J. Rodriguez was there to lift her to safety.

"Congratulations, Shannon Douglas!" the announcer said. "Shannon is the first woman ever to make it to eight on Boilermaker." The JumboTron cut to the cowboy ready area where C.J. twirled Shannon in his arms. If Dixie didn't know better she'd guess the pair was a couple, but Shannon was too smart to attach herself to a womanizing cowboy like C.J.

"Let's see what the judges think of Shannon's ride." The fans kept their gazes glued to the JumboTron. "An eighty-two! Not bad for an eight-second day at the office."

"Shannon was amazing. She deserves better than an eighty-two," Dixie said.

"I agree."

"You do?"

"I'm not stupid enough to disagree with a pregnant lady."

His smile was so innocent and sweet Dixie couldn't help but laugh. "Don't poke fun at me, Gavin Tucker."

He slapped a hand over his chest. "I would never tease a preg—"

She elbowed him in the ribs. "Cut it out with the pregnant-lady jokes."

Gavin nuzzled her ear. "Shannon might be the best female bull rider in Arizona, but no one looks as sexy as you do on the back of a bull."

Thrilled but embarrassed by the compliment, Dixie buried her face against Gavin's shirt. "Maybe one day I'll prove I can make it to eight."

"You're not riding any more bulls in this lifetime."

A red flag waved inside Dixie's head and she pushed away from Gavin. "You're not the boss of me."

"Maybe not but I'm half the boss of him." He placed a hand against her stomach.

The intimate touch rattled Dixie and her words came out in a breathless wheeze. "What if *him* is a *her?*"

"All that matters is the baby is healthy." He sat down and Dixie took her seat. "Just so I understand…you're not really considering competing after the baby's born?" he asked.

"No. My bull riding days are over." Although exciting, the sport was too risky. If anything happened to her who would take care of the baby? God forbid she died unexpectedly and her brothers had to raise their niece or nephew.

Gavin will raise the baby. Would he? They both knew he'd proposed to her out of duty not love. A man like Gavin didn't care to be tied down by a family— or a child.

What if you're wrong?

Dixie ignored the clowns entertaining the crowd and lost herself in thought. What if she did die suddenly and Gavin stepped in to raise their son or daughter? If she and Gavin never married, then he'd be a stranger to his own child. A vision of a sobbing toddler fearful of being left alone with Gavin flashed before her eyes.

Agitated, Dixie twirled the ring on her finger. It had been her bright idea to insist on a trial engagement—mostly because her pride wouldn't accept that the only reason Gavin had spent the night with her had been to escape the clutches of Veronica Patriot.

Don't blame Gavin. You were the one who suggested leaving the bar together.

Dixie refused to argue with herself about who was or wasn't at fault for her and Gavin's predicament. Until now she'd only considered doing what was best for her—not what was in the best interest of the baby. Did she dare change her mind and give marriage to Gavin a real shot—for the baby's sake?

What if she opened her heart to Gavin and after a time fell in love with him—then a few years down the road, he became restless and wanted out of their marriage?

Dixie glanced at Gavin whose attention remained on the cowboys behind the chutes. Waking up every morning and seeing his handsome face resting on the pillow next to her would hardly be torture—not to mention she had none…zero…nada complaints about his lovemaking.

Can you make him happy?

That was the million-dollar question—one she wouldn't know the answer to until she and Gavin hung around more. The baby wasn't due for months—plenty of time to decide if marriage was a real option for them. If, after the baby was born, Dixie believed parting ways was best...so be it. Gavin would be none the wiser. Shoving her worries aside, Dixie allowed herself to enjoy the rest of the day in the company of a handsome cowboy.

"Folks, we're takin' a thirty-minute break before the women's barrel racin' event. Check out the live band near the food court and for those of you who haven't tasted the best churro in Arizona, stop by Rosie's, she's givin' away free samples."

Gavin chuckled as the stands cleared. Food sampling was a hit at small-town rodeos. "Are you hungry?" he asked Dixie.

"We ate hotdogs less than an hour ago." Her blue eyes twinkled. "Unless you think because I'm pregnant I'm starving all the time."

"I have no clue how the pregnant female body works." He grinned. "Give me a heads-up when you're getting hungry so I can feed you before you become cranky."

"Ha-ha. Be happy you won't be making midnight runs to the grocery store to pacify my cravings."

Gavin marveled at the change in Dixie's usual stubborn demeanor. He liked the teasing, lighthearted girl. When she shifted in her seat, Gavin asked, "Want to stretch your legs?"

"Let's see if we can find Shannon."

They left the stands and headed to the livestock barns. "This is my favorite time of the year," Dixie said.

A cowboy walking a palomino blocked their path and Gavin pulled Dixie out of the way. After the coast was clear they continued walking. He waited for Dixie to release his hand—she didn't. He tightened his hold on her fingers as they strolled past the horse stalls and admired the bucking stock. "Why do you like autumn so much?"

"The middle of October kicks off the start of the pecan harvest," Dixie said.

"How long does the harvest last?"

"Some years up until Christmas. If my grandfather had difficulty hiring seasonal workers, then me and my brothers stayed home from school and picked pecans."

"Did that happen often…not having enough help during harvest?"

"Johnny said way back in the day when our mother was a baby that my grandfather hired fifty or more pickers each harvest. I guess there were times when he had to turn families away."

"Your grandfather must have been a good man to work for."

"When Mexicans searching for agricultural work crossed the border they hiked straight to Stagecoach and Grandpa's farm."

"Did your grandfather use illegal immigrants as laborers?"

"I'm sure some of them were. Border security wasn't the hot topic then that it is today."

Growing up in Phoenix, Gavin was used to the TV news reporting sting operations to weed out undocumented workers. "I'm still surprised the authorities didn't stop at the farm to check the workers' green cards."

"Grandpa and Grandma treated the migrant workers very well and the families always returned to Mexico after the harvest. I think the sheriff and his deputies focused their attention on real criminals."

"I didn't notice any migrant-worker cabins on the farm." Then again Gavin had only walked through part of the orchard the afternoon he'd come upon Dixie using a tree trunk for target practice.

"The families slept outside in tents. Grandpa rigged up an outdoor latrine and shower and Grandma Ada gave the women her homemade bath soap, which I'm sure they loved."

The mention of Grandma Ada's soaps reminded Gavin of the surprise waiting for Dixie in Yuma. "Did you want to stay and watch your brothers compete this afternoon?"

"I guess so, why?"

"I was hoping to leave early. There's something I want to show you."

"That's fine. My brothers won't care if I'm cheering them on or not."

"Okay, then. Let's say goodbye to Shannon and be on our way."

Gavin and Dixie left the barn and returned to the cowboy ready area behind the chutes. They weaved through the throng of rodeo personnel until they found Shannon talking to a reporter. They hung back, waiting for the cowgirl to finish the interview. When the reporter left, Dixie caught Shannon's attention.

"Congratulations, Shannon," Dixie said.

The women hugged and then Shannon glanced at Gavin. "Thanks for bringing Dixie today."

"Sure thing. That was a hell of a ride."

"Yeah, it was, wasn't it?" Shannon's smile widened.

"What's up with the little show you and C. J. Rodriguez put on for the audience?" Dixie asked.

"Wrangler wants us to travel together for the next year and compete in the same rodeos."

"Why?"

"The production managers want the fans to believe there's a romance between me and C.J. because they think it will increase ticket sales." Shannon lowered her voice. "I'm not complaining. What girl wouldn't want to travel the circuit with C.J.?"

Dixie ignored Gavin's grin and said, "C.J.'s a player."

"I know what they say about cowboys—"

"What's that?" Gavin interrupted Shannon.

"You can't trust 'em to stick around longer than the time it takes their horse to drink from a water trough," Dixie answered for her friend.

"No worries. Things between me and C.J. are friendly but not too friendly. He just broke up with a barrel racer from California. He won't admit it, but he's nursing a broken heart."

"Be careful, Shannon."

"I will." The women hugged and Shannon strolled off.

Gavin took Dixie's hand and they left the building. Once they reached his truck, he said, "What I want to show you is in Yuma. Mind if we grab supper there instead of stopping on the way?"

"Sounds good." Dixie hopped into the front seat and fastened her belt then yawned. Five minutes later, she was fast asleep.

GAVIN PARKED IN FRONT of a cinder-block single story home at the end of Main Street in Yuma. A banner reading Sold had been slapped across the For Sale sign in the window. Heart pumping with excitement he gently shook Dixie awake. "We're here."

Dixie's eyelashes fluttered up and she straightened in the seat. "Where's here?" She glanced out her window.

"Dixie's Desert Delights."

Her brow scrunched. "What are you talking about?"

He nodded to the vacant house.

"I don't get it. We're parked in front of an ugly, run-down home that's..." Dixie looked at Gavin with wide eyes—like a child who'd caught a glimpse of Santa Claus sneaking up the chimney. "You bought this property?"

Gavin grinned. "Yep." He hopped out of the truck, skirted the hood, then opened her door and helped her out. They stood on the sidewalk and studied the cracked window at the front of the house.

"It's not in great shape, but with your brothers' help, we'll give it a face-lift. You'll have to decide on a paint color for the outside." He walked to the front door and inserted the key then flipped on the lights and stood back.

In a trancelike state Dixie stepped inside and spun in a slow circle.

Gavin crossed the room and stood before a crumbling adobe fireplace. "The Realtor said you might have to do some extra advertising to draw people down here to the end of the block." Dixie's mouth hung open as she wandered about the room.

"There's a bathroom and a small kitchen that will come in handy for making your soaps." When Dixie remained silent, Gavin became nervous. "The original owners sold the house in the late fifties when the property was zoned for business. Through the years it's functioned as a coffee shop, an antiques store and a lawyer's office, but the past four years it sat empty."

Dixie's face remained a blank slate and the excitement Gavin had felt all day fizzled. "What's the matter? You don't like the place?"

"I don't understand, Gavin." Her voice broke, his name escaping her mouth in three syllables.

What did she not understand? He crossed the room and stood before her. "This is where you're going to sell your soaps."

"Why…how…when—"

He pressed a finger against her lips. "Why…because you're the mother of my child. How…I had money saved up, which I used for a down payment. When…I contacted a Realtor last week and she showed me the house. I thought it could easily be turned into a gift shop."

"What was the down payment?"

"Don't worry, I'm not destitute." He chuckled. "You won't have to support me."

"This isn't funny, Gavin."

"I didn't buy this property to make you cry."

"No, you did this because you felt sorry for me, didn't you?" Dixie backed up a step. "Stupid Dixie gets taken to the cleaners by an online scammer and—"

"I never said you were stupid."

"But you thought it." She wiped a tear from her cheek. "I don't know where I'm going to get the money to pay you back."

"I don't want to be paid back." Gavin wouldn't allow Dixie's pride to stand in the way of him helping her.

"I can't accept this as a gift."

Thinking quick on his feet, Gavin said, "I didn't buy this for you, Dixie. I bought this for the baby, so our child would have the security he or she deserves." Sort of the truth…in a roundabout way.

"What do you mean?"

"I agreed to pay child support but I wanted you to have a means of supporting yourself."

"I've taken care of myself since my grandmother passed away. I don't need you or—"

"Before you say anything more, check out the place. If you don't believe this will work for a gift shop then I'll have the Realtor put the property back on the market."

She gasped. "You already signed the papers?"

He nodded.

Dixie looked away first. Gavin wished he knew what was going on in her pretty head, but he stood there like a dope, waiting for her to make the next move. She did—in the direction of the kitchen. Gavin remained in the front room.

Way to go, idiot. He'd expected his gift to make Dixie happy. Instead, he'd upset her. Gavin shuffled to the front window and glanced down the block. The streetlights had come on and local businesses were locking their doors.

Had he misread the situation? He'd sworn he'd heard passion and excitement in Dixie's voice when she'd told him about her plans to market her grandmother's soaps. He'd thought for sure she'd be thrilled to manage her own business.

"Gavin?" Dixie's silhouette darkened the kitchen doorway.

"What?"

"It's perfect."

Chest aching with relief, he said, "Good. Because your brothers are meeting me here tomorrow and we're working on the place."

Dixie moved toward him and he met her in the middle of the room. "I'll help, too," she said.

"You'll be busy making soap." He cupped her cheek. "You need inventory before you open a business."

"You're right. I'll need to stock up on supplies and, oh, there's a new soap mold in a catalog I've been eyeing. Then Christmas is right around the corner and—"

Gavin leaned in and kissed Dixie. He'd wanted to kiss her all day. He intended to keep it light and innocent but Dixie hugged him, pressing her breasts to his chest and he lost all self-control. He backed her up against the wall and nudged his thigh between her legs. She moaned, her arms squeezing his neck harder when he threaded his fingers through her hair. He could have kissed her forever if he hadn't needed air to breathe. Gasping, he pulled away. "Everything will work out, Dixie. You'll see."

Chapter Nine

"I don't know what to say." Dixie clung to Gavin. She never expected to sell her grandmother's soaps in a boutique—that's why she'd attempted to start an internet business. After being scammed out of five-thousand dollars she'd believed her promise to her grandmother would never be realized. Now Gavin was bringing her dream back to life in an amazing way.

In light of his kindness, how could she not give Gavin the benefit of the doubt and try to make their relationship work? Of course there were risks involved—mainly to her heart. Dixie slammed the door on her negative thoughts. She'd spent an entire day with Gavin and not once had she wished to be anywhere else. Not once had she worried about her and the baby's future or how she intended to support herself. With Gavin by her side she felt secure and safe. She tightened her hold and kissed his cheek, his five o'clock shadow tickling her nose.

Gavin threaded his fingers through her hair, and holding her head in place he plunged his tongue into her mouth. Lord, the cowboy could kiss. *Careful...* She'd best move slowly with Gavin or physical desire would shove aside common sense and she'd fall head over heels in love. Then where would she be if he changed his mind about her and the baby and decided he wanted nothing to do with them?

The reservations still existed—a part of her feared Gavin wouldn't always be there for her and their child—but buying this property proved he wanted to make her happy. Clinging to that scrap of hope Dixie decided the only surefire way to know if Gavin was with her for the long haul was to stop throwing roadblocks in his way and open her heart to him.

He broke off the kiss. "We'd better slow down, honey."

"I don't want to." She locked gazes with him, hoping he'd read the sincerity in her eyes.

"I didn't buy this property to coax you into my bed," he said.

"This has nothing to do with the shop." *And everything to do with giving our baby...us...a chance to be a real family.*

Gavin dipped his head and kissed her neck. "If and when we make love, it won't be against a wall or on the hard floor."

"Let's go back to the farm."

"And have your brothers stand outside your bedroom door eavesdropping?" He nuzzled her neck.

Gavin was right—her brothers would be a problem. "What about the barn?"

He grinned. "How many gentlemen friends have you entertained in the hayloft?"

"You'd be the first." Gavin was the first man she'd slept with who was skilled in bed, and unlike her mother's boyfriends he hadn't run from his responsibility.

"I'm tempted to roll in the hay with you, but we can't forget the baby. You've had a long day and need a good night's sleep."

Dixie dropped her gaze before Gavin read the disappointment in her eyes. How were they supposed to grow closer if he always thought of the baby before her? Determined to give it one more try, she stood on tiptoes and poured her heart and soul into her kiss.

Gavin responded with gusto, snuggling her body against his arousal. But a few seconds later he stepped back and winked. "Once this place is fixed up, we'll christen it properly."

Heart breaking, Dixie said, "I'm going to hold you to your promise."

"Honey, that's one promise I intend to keep."

"Well if it isn't the newest entrepreneur in town."

The unenthusiastic statement greeted Dixie Monday morning when she stopped in at Ed's Graphic and Design, a printing shop on Main Street in Yuma. "Hello, Mrs. Hinkle."

Mildred Hinkle owned the Penny Saver Market across the street from Susie's Souvenirs. Last year she'd asked Mrs. Hinkle if she'd sell Dixie's organic soaps in her store but the old woman had snubbed her nose at Dixie's request.

"I hear you plan to sell those little soaps you make in that run-down hovel at the end of the street." Mildred frowned, her wrinkled mouth drawing into a pucker.

Only two days had passed since Gavin had revealed his surprise—darned if Dixie would allow Mrs. Hinkle to put a damper on her excitement. "Yes, I'm turning the house into a gift shop." And since she had more space than she needed for just the soaps, Dixie planned to experiment with other products and develop a line of bath salts and lotions as well as doing custom-made gift baskets. She was even considering offering do-it-yourself classes on organic soap-making.

"Have you decided on a name for your business?" Ed, the owner of the printing shop stepped from the back room.

"I have." She smiled at the tall, middle-age man. "Dixie's Desert Delights."

"That sounds right nice."

Dixie ignored Mildred's scoff.

"I'm guessing you're here to order a sign to hang out front of your business," Ed said.

"I was hoping—"

"Make sure she follows the rules the chamber of commerce created," Mrs. Hinkle interrupted. "Your sign has to be the same size as the rest of the businesses along Main Street." She gathered her sales flyers and marched out the door.

"Don't pay attention to Mildred. She doesn't want anyone's business outshining hers."

Dixie hadn't considered that other merchants might view her as a threat. She guessed with the struggling economy that most people were pinching pennies and local businesses had to compete for customers.

"I hear your brothers are busy sprucing up the place."

"The inspection report on the property wasn't bad," Dixie said. "The wiring has to be updated, but the structure itself is sound."

Ed pulled out a three-ring binder from beneath the counter. "What kind of sign are you interested in and what's your budget?"

"I was thinking of a design that resembled one of my gift-wrapped soaps." She removed a bar from her coat pocket.

Ed studied the soap. "It's doable. What colors did you have in mind?"

"The cinder block is being painted an olive-green so I thought rose for the tissue paper color and buttercream for the bow."

"Black lettering?" Ed asked.

"No, chocolate-brown."

"That'll work. After I create the design you can make any last-minute changes."

"Do I have a choice of font styles?"

Ed flipped through the binder, then spun the book toward Dixie.

After perusing the pages, she pointed to a script she believed her grandmother would have approved of. "I like this one." There was a touch of feminine flourish to each letter yet the font was bold, clean and readable.

"I'll have this finished by the end of the business day tomorrow."

"And the cost?"

"Depends on the size," Ed said.

"Mrs. Hinkle said the sign had to be the same dimensions as others along the block."

"That's just Mildred bellyaching. You can have any size sign you want."

"What about the chamber of commerce? I can't afford a fine."

"The only rule the chamber enforces is that a business sign can't block a traffic light. Other than that buy whatever size you can afford."

"Since I'm the farthest away from the middle of town I'd like the biggest sign."

"That'll run you twelve hundred. Included in the price are the poles and hardware to attach it to the shop and a special UV coating to prevent the colors from fading in the sun."

Twelve hundred was a lot of money. "I'll think about it and let you know when I stop in tomorrow to view the design."

"Sure thing."

"Thanks, Ed." Dixie left the print shop and strolled down the block, studying the signs hanging outside each business. When she reached Dixie's Desert Delights she decided she needed to purchase the largest sign. The twelve hundred dollars would have to go on her credit card.

"Watch out." Johnny rounded the corner of the house, carrying a load of two-by-fours. She followed him inside.

Her brothers and Gavin had made remarkable progress in less than forty-eight hours and the once neglected house was becoming a quaint little gift shop. Fresh paint, repairs to the fireplace and new shelving mounted on the walls gave the inside a cozy feel. "Where's Gavin?" she asked after Johnny laid the boards on the floor.

"Outside talking to the plumber."

The last she'd heard, the toilet flushed fine. "What's wrong with the plumbing?"

"Not sure." Johnny nodded to the pile of wood. "Where do you want the counter for the cash register?"

"By the back wall facing the front door."

"Makes sense." Johnny began taking measurements. "When Merle gets here send him over to the hardware store. Gavin's got an order of supplies waiting to be picked up." Johnny finished measuring, then left to fetch another load of wood.

Our dream is coming true, Grandma.

"Hey, you're here." Gavin stepped through the kitchen doorway wearing no shirt and a tool belt slung low on his jean-clad hips. If rodeo didn't work out for him he'd make a sexy handyman. He grinned when he caught her staring and her pulse skipped a beat.

"I ordered a sign for the front of the shop." As if Gavin sported a huge magnet glued to his chest, Dixie's feet glided across the floor. She stopped before him and brushed at an imaginary speck of dirt sticking to his sweaty shoulder. Her fingers lingered longer than necessary—ever since she'd decided to give her relationship with Gavin a real chance, she couldn't resist touching him.

"Porter and Buck took off." Gavin's gaze fastened onto Dixie's mouth and she swayed closer.

Mesmerized by his dark eyes, she said, "That wasn't nice of them to leave you shorthanded."

"I asked Buck to keep Porter busy. Your brother means well but he can't hammer nails worth a damn."

"I'll help you."

"Thanks, but I don't want to take any chance of you hurting yourself."

There he went...worrying about the baby.

"Once the shop is finished, you'll be busy setting up your inventory." He stroked a finger across her cheek and her skin tingled at the simple caress. "Have lunch with me."

Hypnotized by his brown eyes Dixie nodded. The batch of cinnamon-citrus soap waiting in the barn back at the farm could wait a while longer. "I'll grab sandwiches from the deli across the street."

"Give me a half hour." He kissed the tip of her nose and walked off, leaving her yearning for more. When she turned away she caught Johnny spying at the front door.

"Why the change of heart?" her brother asked.

"What are you talking about?"

"You and Gavin. You're acting lovey-dovey all of a sudden. A week ago you bristled when he got too close."

Dixie wasn't about to share her feelings with her brother.

"You two decide on a wedding date?" Johnny asked.

A few days ago Dixie would have balked at going through with a wedding. Now the ceremony was a real possibility. "Not yet." She crinkled her nose. "You'll be the first to know when we do." She stopped at the door. "I'm off to the deli."

"I'll take a—"

"Sorry, you're on your own for lunch." She closed the front door behind her, ignoring her brother's scowl.

Thirty minutes later, deli food in hand, Dixie entered the backyard behind the shop. She placed the food on a stone wall beneath the shade of a piñon tree and waited for Gavin to join her.

"Thanks for getting lunch." He sat next to her and she handed him a sandwich.

"Are you antsy yet?" Dixie opened a bag of chips.

"Antsy about what?"

"Returning to rodeo."

Gavin considered Dixie's question, then answered honestly. "I haven't given rodeo much thought the past few days." He'd been so involved in whipping the property into shape that he hadn't had time to miss busting broncs. Was it possible that the incessant urgency he felt to push himself to the limits dissipated when he focused on making Dixie happy? Rodeo had been the vehicle of choice to feed his addiction to danger after he'd left the army. The fact that lately he hadn't felt the need to take risks gave Gavin pause.

He reflected on the previous night when he and Dixie had worked side by side in the shop. The mellow sounds of country music had played on the radio while Dixie painted a stencil on the wall and Gavin tiled the bathroom floor. There'd been no need for conversation—both of them comfortable with the silence. Gavin had never felt more at peace with himself than when he was with Dixie. Since the rodeo in Bullhead City the intensity of his nightmares had tapered off. There was no doubt in his mind that Dixie was good for his soul.

"You must be tired after having to sleep on the blowup mattress."

Dixie had loaned him the mattress so he could stay at the shop and work late into the night, then wake at the crack of dawn and begin all over again. "You won't hear any complaints from me. It beats sleeping on the hard ground."

There were times in Afghanistan when he and his men had been forced to sleep in their bedrolls on the rocky soil. Dixie had offered to give up her bedroom at the farm but Gavin insisted she needed a good night's rest more than he did. To tell the truth he thought she was pushing herself too hard.

"Maybe you should head home after lunch and take a nap."

"I can't afford to rest. I need to make more soap."

"You have to think about the baby, Dixie."

She stiffened and for the life of Gavin he couldn't figure out why she bristled each time he mentioned the baby. Wasn't a father supposed to show interest in his child?

Although she didn't look pregnant, the more time he spent with Dixie the more real the baby became. Last night Gavin had lain in the dark and envisioned buying a home in Yuma. Dixie and the baby would head to the gift shop each morning and Gavin would drive to a civilian job. At the end of the day their little family would eat a cozy meal followed by a long walk through the neighborhood—Gavin pushing the stroller.

The midnight musing should have caused a panic attack because settling down threatened his plan to stay on the move and keep one step ahead of the memories of Nate's death.

You've hardly thought of Nate the past few weeks.

The realization shook Gavin. Nate had been more than a friend—he'd been a brother. *Nate wouldn't want you to feel guilty over his death.* Yeah, well, Nate hadn't seen the look in his mother's eyes when Gavin had stopped at her home to deliver the few possessions Nate had accumulated while in the army.

"Have you given any thought to baby names?" Dixie asked.

"No, have you?"

"If it's a girl I'd like to name her after my grandmother." Dixie peeked at Gavin. "But Ada's old-fashioned."

"Is Ada short for anything?"

"Adelle. My grandmother's people were French."

"Adelle is a nice name. Maybe we could call her Addy instead of Ada."

"I like that."

"I have a suggestion for a boy's name," Gavin said.

"As long as it isn't a country-western singer."

Gavin chuckled. "I was hoping…if you agreed… maybe naming him after my buddy Nate." Gavin couldn't go back in time and save his friend but he could honor Nate's memory by naming his son after him.

"Nathan. That's a nice strong name," she said.

"You're sure?"

"Positive."

Changing the subject, Gavin asked, "Are you planning a grand opening for the shop?"

"I guess I should," Dixie mumbled.

"What's the matter?" Gavin snagged her hand and rubbed the callused pad of his thumb across her knuckles. "Having doubts about managing your own business?"

"No." She sighed. "I'm worried I won't sell enough inventory to pay the mortgage."

"My child-support checks will make up the difference if sales fall short."

"It's going to be difficult to watch the store and keep up with making new products."

"You'll figure out a way." With Johnny's help Gavin had poured a cement slab in the backyard for the potbelly stove, which they'd brought from the barn and hooked up yesterday. "What else is troubling you?"

"Susie gave me the cold shoulder when I picked up the rest of my soaps from her shop."

"You're her competition now."

"I guess, but I worry that you wasted your money, Gavin. Dixie's Desert Delights is just one of several gift shops along Main Street. What if I don't make enough money to reimburse you for the down payment?"

"I don't want to be reimbursed." He threaded his fingers through hers. "We should set a wedding date and tie the knot before the baby's born." Gavin hated the thought of his child being labeled a bastard, but the desire to marry Dixie had more to do with making Gavin feel safe. With Dixie by his side there was hope that he'd conquer the demons chasing him and live a normal, fulfilling life—as normal as possible for a soldier returning from the war front.

Fearing if he revealed the truth behind his proposal, Dixie would run for the hills, he focused on what was best for the baby, not him. "Most people today don't give a hoot if a couple marries before, after or if ever once the baby's born, but I care, Dixie. I want to be married to the mother of my child before my son or daughter makes an entrance into the world."

"I thought—"

"I realize we're still feeling our way as a couple, but I hope I've proved my intentions are sincere."

"You have."

"Then pick a date."

"What about your rodeo schedule? Would you continue to ride after the baby's born?"

"That depends," he said.

"On what?"

"On whether or not you want to make this a real marriage."

Chapter Ten

"Dixie, I swear I've never smelled anything better than this." Skylar Riggins held up a bar of soap from Dixie's Christmas collection.

"That's one of my favorites." The Christmas-tree-shaped bar spawned fond memories of Dixie and her grandmother experimenting with herbs and oils in the barn. The Christmas before her grandmother had passed away they'd worked on a new holiday scent, and when Dixie had suggested adding nutmeg to the recipe her grandmother had hugged her and said with pride, "I'll rest easy knowing my recipes will be in good hands."

"Have you seen my new romance line?" Dixie nodded to the decorative hatbox brimming with delicate heart-shaped pink and peach soaps. While Skylar walked off to do more sniffing, Dixie milled about the customers—all women—attending Dixie's Desert Delights Grand Opening Saturday afternoon.

Gavin and her brothers had worked tirelessly all week to ready the shop for business and Dixie had spent endless hours making soap and putting up flyers in town advertising the event. Next to the front door she'd placed a basket of soap samples and a gift certificate to a local restaurant to be given away in a drawing to one lucky customer who stopped by the store today. Dixie couldn't have asked for a better turnout and was surprised and pleased when the gals she'd rodeoed with this past summer had showed up to support her.

"Dixie," Hannah Buck spoke from across the room. "Do you have any soap for men?"

The question caught the attention of several women. "I do." Dixie opened the glass door of her grandmother's dining-room hutch and pointed to the bars on the top shelf. "The scents are called Bad Boy, Charmer, Swashbuckler and Cowboy." Several women rushed over to examine the products.

"My favorite is Cowboy," Dixie said. After smelling Gavin's cologne all week she'd been inspired to create a line of soap for men. Cowboy contained a hint of sandalwood and musk.

"Mmm. Sexy. I'll take a Cowboy and a Bad Boy." The woman winked at Dixie. "Either of these will be an improvement over what's waiting for me at home."

"Dare I ask who's waiting at home?" Dixie smiled.

"The mailman." The women laughed.

"You think that's bad, I've got a mechanic at my house."

Dixie took Hannah by the elbow and led her to the checkout counter. She nodded at the soap in her friend's hand. "Who's the lucky guy?"

"I don't want to jinx anything but I met this really nice guy at work and I think he likes me except…" Hannah waved a hand in the air. "Never mind."

"What she's not saying—" Kim Beaderman joined the women at the counter "—is that this really nice guy is my brother."

Dixie waggled an eyebrow. "Sounds like a soap opera…*As the Yuma Medical Center Turns*."

"Mike and I are just friends," Hannah insisted, her cheeks turning pink.

Dixie gave Hannah the sale's slip to sign. "Thanks for coming by today. I was worried about a poor turn-out."

Kim waved a hand. "The place is packed. Your store's a hit."

"I hope things stay this way through Christmas." She pointed to the raffle gift by the door. "Don't forget to fill out your email address for the drawing."

The women walked off, and Dixie turned her attention to the front window. Each time she caught a glimpse of Gavin using his cowboy charm to hawk her soaps and entice women into her shop, Dixie's heart melted.

Instead of heading off to a rodeo, Gavin had remained in Yuma for her grand opening. Last night her brothers had informed her that they were competing in Payson today, so when Gavin waltzed into the store this morning with breakfast burritos and orange juice she'd been caught off guard. He'd done so much for her already and she'd felt guilty he'd passed up a rodeo to stay behind and help her. Although she insisted she could handle the opening by herself, Dixie was secretly grateful for Gavin's support.

"So..." Wendy Chin slipped behind the counter and hugged Dixie. "I hear congratulations are in order." Wendy's gaze dropped to Dixie's stomach. "When's the baby due?"

"March."

"How are things between you and the baby's father?" Wendy nodded to the front window.

"We're fine. Why?"

"Judging by the way Gavin ogled you a few minutes ago I'd say you two are more than fine."

Gavin had been watching her?

"He was staring at you like a serial killer eyes his next victim."

Dixie gaped.

Wendy flashed a cheeky grin. "I don't read romance books. I read thrillers. It was meant as a compliment."

"Gavin's a great guy." No matter how things turned out between them, Dixie would always hold him in high regard. "He's been a huge help—"

"Oh, yeah, I bet he has." Wendy laughed.

"What's so funny?" Julie Kenner asked.

Dixie moved from behind the counter and hugged Julie. "Thanks for stopping in."

"Sorry, I'm late. I had to work a half day." Julie motioned to the crowd of women. "The store looks great, Dixie. I can't believe you opened your own business."

"I couldn't have done this without Gavin's help." Dixie spied him chatting with Mildred Hinkle. He handed her a soap sample and darned if he didn't make the old biddy blush.

"Excuse me a minute." Dixie cut through the crowd. "Hello, Mrs. Hinkle," she said when Mildred stepped through the door. "Nice of you to drop by. While you're browsing help yourself to cookies and punch in the kitchen."

"Never mind refreshments. That nice young man out front told me if I use this—" she held up a sample from Dixie's romance collection "—my Walden's headaches will completely disappear."

Dixie swallowed a laugh, then guided Mildred to the pink hatbox. "Use any of these soaps from my romance collection and Walden won't be able to keep his hands off you."

"The sign in the window says you'll refund my money or offer an exchange if I don't like the soap."

"That's right. Return it and—"

"You want customers to bring back used soap?"

"I certainly do. Have you heard of Clean the World?" Mildred shook her head. "Clean the World is a soap recycling program that collects bars of used soap and distributes them to needy communities all over the world."

"How awful to give someone dirty soap."

Dixie laughed. "All the used bars are run through a sanitization process first."

"Hmm. Never heard of the group but I guess it's nice to help people when you can."

"Why don't you try one bar and if Walden doesn't care for it, exchange the soap for a different scent until you find his favorite."

"All right. I'll do that." Mildred handed Dixie a bar wrapped in rose-colored ribbon and followed her to the cash register. "Is that young man outside related to you?"

Dixie didn't want Mildred to know that she and Gavin were engaged. If things didn't work out between them she'd have to answer the woman's nosy questions. "He's a friend."

"Well, you should work harder at making him more than a friend, young lady. Men like him don't come along often."

Dixie couldn't agree more. She handed Mildred her change and gift bag. "Thank you for stopping in, Mrs. Hinkle."

"You're welcome, dear."

Dear? There went another reason Dixie needed Gavin—he converted her enemies to friends.

"Hey, Dixie, we're heading over to the Dude Ranch if you and Gavin want to stop by later," Hannah said. The Dude Ranch was a saloon, which featured local country music bands and a huge dance floor.

"Maybe next time." Dixie hadn't gone out with the girls in forever—since the Boot Hill Rodeo in July, but her dogs were barking and the day wasn't over.

"Don't be a party-pooper, Dix," Shannon said. "Next week I'm heading to Florida with C.J. I won't be back for at least a month."

"Thanks for the invite, but it's been a long week." Not to mention she couldn't drink alcohol and she wasn't in the mood for loud music and greasy buffalo wings. Her gaze drifted to the window. With her brothers away at a rodeo she had the house to herself tonight. What really appealed to her was soft music and sharing the porch swing with Gavin.

"Take care, Dixie," Skylar said. The rest of the gang waved goodbye and left.

Three hours until closing.

Three hours until she was alone with Gavin.

GAVIN STOOD BY THE DOOR watching Dixie straighten the gift shop for tomorrow's crowd. She looked frazzled, tired but happy. Her stomach growled and he chuckled. "I heard that all the way over here. C'mon. You need to eat."

"I want to get things ready for tomorrow."

While Dixie locked up the cash and credit card receipts in the small safe Gavin had installed in a kitchen cupboard, he mulled over the day. He knew diddly-squat about women's buying habits and fancy-smelling soaps but he'd kept track of the number of people who'd visited the shop with his handy dandy counter gadget. If half the hundred-thirty-two customers purchased a bar of soap then the grand opening of Dixie's Desert Delights had been a success.

"Okay, I'm ready." Dixie flashed a tired smile as she put on her coat.

Gavin held the door for her, then took the key from her fingers and secured the lock.

"I'm not so tired that I'm unable to lock the door," she grumbled.

He handed her the key. "I locked the outside shed earlier."

"I forgot about the shed. I'm used to leaving the barn doors wide-open and not worrying about thieves."

Gavin grasped Dixie's elbow and escorted her to the side of the house where he'd parked his truck. "This area of downtown seems safe but I wouldn't test your luck and leave the doors or shed unlocked."

"I promise I'll be more vigilant."

He helped Dixie into his truck and slid onto the driver's seat. "What are you hungry for?"

"Anything."

Gavin had ordered a sandwich for Dixie at noon and had had it delivered to the shop but he doubted she'd eaten it. He refrained from lecturing her about taking better care of herself for the baby's sake because he didn't want to ruin what had been a great day for her. He opened his mouth to suggest a nice meal at a sit-down restaurant but Dixie yawned. "We'll stop at the drive-through in Stagecoach and grab a couple of burgers to go. How does that sound?"

"Great." Dixie slouched into a comfortable position.

"Go ahead and turn on the radio—" she yawned again "—while I rest my eyes for a minute."

She was fast asleep before Gavin left Yuma city limits. He switched on the radio, lowering the volume, then sang along in his head with Kenny Chesney. The city lights faded to black in the rearview mirror and snoring sounds escaped from Dixie's mouth. She looked soft and kissable.

Gavin gripped the wheel tighter and willed his libido to cool. This past week he'd woken each morning with a hard-on. Shoot, he hadn't been this horny since the age of thirteen when he'd wanted to kiss Stephanie Quaker in study hall.

Get a grip, man.

He managed to steer his thoughts and the truck onto the county road that led into Stagecoach. He decided not to stop at the drive-through because he hadn't the heart to wake Dixie. They'd scrounge up something to eat at the farm. Fifteen minutes later he turned onto the road to the Cash property. The house was dark when he pulled into the yard. He shut off the truck and set the brake.

Dixie remained sound asleep...tempting him. He unsnapped his belt, leaned across the seat and kissed her neck. She swatted at him but missed. Grinning, he blew in her ear. This time she jumped, the movement sending her shoulder cracking against his jaw.

He rubbed his chin and chuckled. "Ouch."

Dixie blinked. "We're home."

Home. An unfamiliar yearning pulled at Gavin's heartstrings. He hadn't considered anyplace *home* in years. He tried to envision him and Dixie raising a handful of kids with a pecan grove for a backyard. Three months ago his mind would have been a blank slate but now… He could see himself walking out the door and down the porch steps to get in his truck and leave for work.

"You were sleeping so soundly I didn't want to wake you. I thought we could eat here."

"Sure, that's fine." Dixie led the way into the house and into the kitchen. "I haven't had time to grocery shop this week." She opened the fridge door—the shelves were bare.

Gavin peeked over her shoulder. "Any soup in the pantry?"

Dixie confiscated two cans of chicken noodle and a box of saltines. "This won't fill you up."

"Don't worry about me. I'll stop for a snack when I head back to Yuma." Gavin had been making the round-trip every day while they'd worked on the store. He hadn't minded the drive until tonight. Lack of sleep was catching up with him.

"Do you care if I take a quick shower while you heat the soup?" Dixie paused in the doorway. "If I don't grab one now my brothers will use up all the hot water when they return from the rodeo."

"Go ahead." Gavin listened to Dixie's light footfalls on the stairs and closed his eyes, envisioning her naked body standing beneath a spray of water.

The pipes rattled and clanked behind the kitchen wall and Gavin's willpower diminished. He'd kept his hands to himself all week—no easy task when Dixie *accidentally* bumped into him. Or he'd caught her staring at his backside when she thought he wasn't looking.

Dixie wants you as bad as you want her.

They were engaged. What the heck were they waiting for?

Gavin decided to take matters into his own hands.

He didn't know why Dixie hadn't answered him when he'd asked if she'd intended to make their marriage a real one after they tied the knot, but as far as he was concerned, the more *real* their relationship became the better the chances of their marriage succeeding. He climbed the stairs, stopping in the hallway to strip. He left his clothes on the floor outside the door.

Dixie's humming greeted him when he stepped into the bathroom. A light-colored shower curtain enclosed the claw-foot tub and Gavin could see her silhouette through the sheer fabric.

Hoping not to startle her too badly, he slid the curtain aside at the end of the tub and stepped in. Dixie's back faced him, offering a view of her firm little fanny and curvy hips. Arms raised above her head, she shampooed her hair.

Gavin moved closer and braced his hands against the wall on either side of her body, and then he pressed his chest to her back. Dixie gasped, the action causing her to suck in a mouthful of water. She coughed, sputtered and spun. Eyes wide she opened her mouth to speak but Gavin caressed her breasts and instead she moaned. He didn't wait for permission. He nibbled a path across her shoulder, up her neck and ended with a kiss beneath her ear.

"We were supposed to christen the gift shop not the shower." She leaned heavily against him.

"I've been thinking about making love to you all week and when I heard the shower go on…"

Dixie clasped his face between her hands and stood on tiptoe. "Don't stop." She pressed her mouth to Gavin's and ignored the voice in her head insisting she proceed with caution. She wanted no reminders of what happened when she'd allowed her emotions and desires to take the lead. Dixie was tired of pretending she didn't need Gavin.

Right now. Right here. She needed him more than anything. She understood the risks involved in making love, but Gavin had squeaked through her defenses when he'd surprised her with the gift shop. The reasons they shouldn't be a couple no longer mattered. Dixie was willing to risk her heart because she had the baby in her corner. Gavin cared about the baby and the baby was inside her. They were a package deal.

She wiggled closer, loving the feel of his powerful body. She tried to express what he meant to her through kisses and caresses…safer than saying the words out loud. With each touch she intended to show him that she was committed to their relationship. "Please, Gavin."

"I couldn't stop if I wanted to, honey."

"HEY, DIXIE! WHERE'S GAVIN?" Johnny's voice echoed through the upstairs hallway.

Dixie gasped and Gavin clamped a hand over her mouth. She giggled at the stern look he gave her. They'd played in the shower until the cold water had forced them out. Good grief they were both adults having a baby together. So what if her brother caught them naked?

"Dixie?" Johnny pounded on the bathroom door.

Gavin wrapped Dixie in a towel, then tied one around his waist before opening the door. She peeked over Gavin's shoulder. Johnny stood in the hallway holding Gavin's clothes. Before anyone had a chance to speak the rest of her brothers skidded to a stop in the doorway.

"Well, now. That's a cozy sight." Willie expelled a grunt after Buck jabbed an elbow into his stomach.

Poor Buck. Finding his baby sister almost naked with

a man was more than his prudish brain could process. "I didn't expect you until later tonight," she said.

"Obviously." Porter snickered.

Gavin raised his hand. "Before you interrogate your sister, give us some privacy to—"

"The last thing you two need is more privacy." Johnny shoved Gavin's clothes at him. "You're supposed to save that stuff for the honeymoon."

Conway came to Dixie's defense. "She's twenty-three, Johnny. Old enough to have sex. Hell, you were poking Ilene back in ninth grade. She was only—"

"Shut up, Conway."

"No you shut up, Johnny. Just because you're the oldest doesn't mean you can—"

"Hey," Willie interrupted. "Is that why Ilene wouldn't go to the school dance with me when I asked her? Because you were banging her in Grandpa's truck?"

Buck interrupted before Johnny had a chance to defend himself. "Didn't Grandpa find a condom on the floor of the backseat of his truck?"

"Shoot. Grandpa accused *me* of having sex with a girl. All along it was you." Willie shoved his finger in Johnny's chest.

"That was years ago. Besides, you never liked Ilene because she had small…you know." Johnny's face turned red.

"I wouldn't have cared if her boobs were no bigger than pecan nuts if she'd have let me under her skirt," Willie said.

"I thought you were in love with Marsha, Will?" Merle joined the conversation. "You said Marsha was your first love?"

"When did I say that?" Willie argued.

"When you got drunk two years ago and Merle had

to haul your ass out of the bar," Johnny said. "You were foaming at the mouth about some girl named Marsha in your high-school class."

Dixie chanced a peek at Gavin and found him staring at her brothers in fascination. She supposed he'd never seen anything the likes of a Cash brothers' argument. Growing up an only child Gavin had missed out on all the action Dixie had seen in her younger years.

"Are we talking about Marsha Bugler?" Buck asked.

It amazed Dixie that no matter how loud or raucous her brothers became Buck's quiet voice always caught their attention.

"Yeah, that's the Marsha we're talking about. Why?" Johnny asked.

"Marsha and I were friends," Buck said.

"Friends?" Willie scoffed. "She never mentioned you when we were together." Willie's eyes narrowed. "Just how good of friends were you?"

"Good enough that she told me you'd gotten her pregnant."

Dixie gasped and her brothers' jaws dropped. "Is that true?" Johnny asked Willie.

No one spoke a word. Moved a muscle. Or breathed as they waited for Willie's answer.

"It's true."

"How come you didn't tell Grandpa or Grandma?" Dixie asked.

"Marsha told me not to tell anyone because she wasn't going to keep the baby," Willie said.

Dixie rested her hand over her tummy as if to protect her unborn child from her brother's confession.

Like a dark cloud hovering overhead, silence filled the hallway as everyone digested Willie's confession. Then Buck asked, "Do you ever hear from Marsha?"

"No. Why would I? She moved to California."

Without another word, Buck retreated to his room, the sound of his clunking boot heels echoing in the air.

"What's up with Buck?" Willie asked Johnny.

"How should I know?" Johnny pointed at Gavin. "Get dressed and meet me outside." The Cash brothers dispersed...Porter and Merle heading to their rooms, the rest following Johnny downstairs.

Dixie shut the bathroom door and leaned against it. "Sorry about the interruption."

Gavin wasn't. Standing naked, save for a skimpy towel and her long hair dripping wet, Dixie had never looked more appealing. If she didn't leave the bathroom soon, he wouldn't let her. He picked up her clothes from the floor and held them out.

As if sensing Gavin's arousal, Dixie mumbled, "I'll get dressed in my room."

Gavin pulled on his jeans. He caught a glimpse of himself in the mirror above the sink and stared long and hard, seeking answers about his and Dixie's future.

He'd spent a lot of time with Dixie lately and had learned a few things about himself in the process. One—her smile produced tiny twinges in his chest. Two—he knew what she was thinking before she spoke out loud. Three—not an hour in the day went by when he didn't want to kiss her. Four—he hadn't missed riding the circuit as he'd anticipated. Five—he'd learned that if he focused his thoughts on Dixie before he fell asleep, the chances of dreaming of Nate's death greatly decreased.

Tonight with Dixie clinging to him in the shower he admitted that he yearned for her to need him not because he provided her and the baby a sense of security, but because she desired him the way a woman desires a man she loves.

Until now, Gavin hadn't admitted to himself that he'd purchased the shop in Yuma because he'd wanted to be tied to Dixie by more than the baby. He turned away from the mirror and slipped into his shirt. He couldn't regret getting Dixie pregnant, because she and his unborn child had become his anchor. Dixie and the baby made sense when nothing else did.

He shoved his feet into his boots and went outside where he found Johnny waiting on the porch swing with a shotgun resting across his lap.

"Are you going hunting?" Gavin asked.

"As soon as Dixie gets out here we're all taking a drive to visit Reverend Thomas."

Johnny would get no argument from Gavin.

Dixie's brother narrowed his eyes. "You're not leaving Stagecoach until you marry my sister."

"Says who?" Dixie stepped onto the porch and planted her fists on her hips.

"Says me." Johnny stood.

"Over my dead body."

Johnny cocked the rifle. "Fine by me."

"Settle down, you two," Gavin said. Johnny was all bluster but Gavin didn't appreciate Dixie's adamant refusal to marry him. Hadn't their lovemaking in the shower meant anything to her?

"I won't be rushed," Dixie insisted.

Gavin came to her rescue. "I believe your sister would like a real wedding…the kind with a guest list and a reception afterward."

"That takes time to plan," Dixie added.

"You two had better get planning then because there

will be no more hanky-panky in this house until you're married."

"Don't talk stupid, Johnny." Dixie looked at Gavin. "I'm starving." She waltzed off the porch and hopped into Gavin's truck.

"If you string my sister along, Tucker, you'll answer to me and my brothers."

If anyone was doing the stringing, it was Dixie, not Gavin.

Chapter Eleven

"You're awfully quiet," Dixie said.

Gavin bit into his Chicago-style hotdog and shrugged. He'd been lost in thought since they'd pulled into Vern's Drive-In fifteen minutes ago.

"You shouldn't let my brothers get to you."

Easier said than done. After Johnny had accused him of leading Dixie on, Gavin had questioned his intentions toward their sister. On the surface he'd convinced himself marrying Dixie was the right thing to do—the one sure way to step up and accept responsibility for his actions. And he admitted that Dixie had a calming effect on him and made him feel more in control of his emotions and his ability to close himself off from the demons that haunted him at night. But after they'd made love in the shower…he'd felt a strong urge to be a good father and provide his child with a stable, normal upbringing—the opposite of what he and Dixie had experienced. This *urge* was gaining steam inside Gavin and scaring him.

What if he didn't turn out to be a good father? "My dad was never in the picture when I was a kid." Hell, Gavin didn't know the first thing about a father's role in the family.

"Did you have any contact with him?" she asked.

"Once. I was fourteen and he scared the crap out of me."

"What happened?"

"I was waiting at a bus stop after dark and he approached me." Gavin remembered that Friday night as if it had happened yesterday. His father had been filthy, his clothes torn, his hair hanging in greasy strands over his shoulders. His breath had smelled putrid—like rotting teeth and beer. His father had said, "What's the matter, son? Don't you recognize me?"

"What did your dad want?"

"Money. He was living on the street." Gavin had given him what was in his pocket—four dollars.

"What did your mother say when you got home and told her?"

Gavin hadn't told his mother right away. He'd slipped into his room and sat on the bed, shaking with disgust and fear. When he'd finally confessed to seeing his father, his mom had been furious and concerned for Gavin's safety. "She was upset and she felt bad that I had to see how destitute my father had become."

"How did he get so bad off?"

"He was a drug addict." Gavin got the creeps when he thought about all the times he'd ridden the city buses alone through the years and how his father could have approached him at any time.

"I'm sorry." Dixie gripped his thigh and his muscle warmed. "I know the feeling of not having a father give a damn about you."

Gavin wanted to show his child he cared by being there in person. But a real marriage to Dixie meant he had to stop running for good…forever. No matter what his fears were, Gavin felt compelled to try—for his child's sake.

"Dixie, you do know that when I asked you to marry me it was with the assumption that we were going to live together."

She removed her hand from his leg, leaving behind a chill where her fingers had touched him.

"I don't want to see my kid every other weekend or just when I'm passing through town on my way to a rodeo. I want to be there every day." In order to do that Gavin would have to land a civilian job and put down roots—the very things he swore he'd steer clear of when he'd left the army.

He credited Dixie with the reprieve he'd experienced from the nightmares that had plagued him after returning from Afghanistan, but could he trust the horrible memories to remain at bay forever? He pictured himself lying next to Dixie in bed, holding her close then awakening to her screams because he dreamt she was the enemy and he'd pinned her to the mattress.

"Will you be truthful with me if I ask you a question?" she said.

Gavin nodded.

"Is the real reason you're pushing marriage because of the shop in Yuma?"

"What do you mean?"

Dixie squirmed, her eyes shifting between Gavin and the neon sign above the drive-in. "Are you worried I won't be a good manager and the shop will go bankrupt?"

The thought hadn't entered his mind. "No. If things don't work out between us and we split, the shop remains yours." Gavin believed as long as Dixie had a means of supporting herself and he refrained from interfering she wouldn't worry about him threatening her independence. "I'm not marrying you to take care of you," he said. "I'm marrying you so that our child has a shot at a normal life." If there was such a thing these days.

Dixie's silence worried Gavin. If he pushed her into marriage before she was ready, would she panic and run as soon as they said "I do"? Evil laughter echoed through his head. If anyone ran it would be *him* not Dixie.

"Okay." The quietly spoken word sounded like a fire-cracker exploding inside the truck.

His blood pumped hard through his veins. "Okay what?"

"Okay, I'll set a wedding date. But nothing fancy. I can't afford a big shindig and you've already spent too much money on the gift shop."

"Small suits me fine, but I'd like there to be enough time for my mother to make arrangements to come."

"I forgot about your mother."

"She's eager to meet you."

Dixie worried her lower lip. "I've been without my mother and grandparents for so long I forgot my preg-nancy doesn't just affect us."

"My mother won't interfere in our decisions about the baby if that concerns you."

"Not at all. My grandmother meant the world to me and I want our baby to have a close relationship with your mother."

"How soon can you put a wedding together?"

"What's your rodeo schedule like the next couple of weeks?"

"I can pick and choose." Gavin wasn't rodeoing for the money, that was for sure.

"Today's date is…"

"October 16."

"Would the first Saturday in November work for you and your mother? I'll check with the church to see if it's available."

"I'll phone my mom on the way back to the store tonight."

Dixie smiled. "Why drive back to Yuma just to sleep?"

"I've been doing it all week."

"My brothers caught us taking a shower together. If we tell them we've picked a wedding date they won't care if you share my bed."

The temperature inside the truck shot up ten degrees as Gavin imagined cuddling Dixie in bed. Now that they were committed to going through with a marriage ceremony, there was no reason they couldn't make love whenever and wherever the mood struck. And after their tryst in the bathroom today, Gavin knew without a doubt that Dixie enjoyed making love with him.

"All right. I'll spend the night at the farm." Her brothers would just have to get used to their sister and Gavin sneaking off to be alone—at least until they decided where they'd live after the wedding. *Don't forget about finding a job.*

Gavin would begin looking for civilian work once he and Dixie were legally married. They'd need time to become used to marriage and living together. He wouldn't push her to find an apartment in Yuma until the baby came and he quit rodeo. He ate the last bite of hotdog, then started the engine and backed out of the parking spot. "I think we should tell your family together," he said.

"That's fine. You can do all the talking."

This was one time Gavin looked forward to confronting the Cash brothers.

"I MADE A TO-DO LIST for the wedding." Conway's abrupt statement as he waltzed into the kitchen Monday morning startled a drowsy Dixie as she ate her oatmeal.

The instant Gavin had announced that they'd selected Saturday, November 4 for their wedding her slick-talking, bucking-bronc rodeo-junky brothers had morphed into wedding planners.

"I want a quiet, family-only ceremony." Dixie shoved her empty bowl across the table and suppressed the growing anxiety that she'd made a mistake in agreeing to a wedding date. Then she remembered the shower she and Gavin had shared two days ago and her heart sighed.

"What's up with the dreamy look on your face?" Conway poured himself a mug of coffee and joined Dixie at the table.

"Sleepy, not dreamy. I wish I could catch a nap before heading into Yuma to open the shop."

"How come Gavin left early this morning?"

Gavin had slept on the sofa and risen at the crack of dawn. She smiled at the memory of him sneaking into her bedroom and waking her with a kiss and a whispered, "I'll call you later."

"Gavin's off rodeoing."

"Where? The next event's in Casa Grande."

"He mentioned California." Dixie assumed Gavin needed some space before they got married in a couple of weeks and she also appreciated the breathing room.

"When will he be back?" Conway asked.

"He didn't say."

"Guess it doesn't matter. You can call him for his opinion on wedding themes."

Themes? "Conway, what are you up to?"

"Your wedding has to have a theme and since you own a soap shop I thought we'd use bubbles."

Dixie sputtered. "Bubbles?" Good Lord, if Conway gave each guest a bottle of bubbles the inside of the church would look like a wash machine gone wild.

"No bubbles," she said. "Besides, we don't have the money for anything extravagant, so the guest list is limited to a handful."

Conway frowned. "I suppose that means the reception has to be at the farm?"

"We'll clean the barn and set up tables in there. Cook barbecue and—"

Conway snapped his fingers. "A pig roast—what a great idea, sis."

"No pigs on a spit!" She winced and lowered her voice. "Pulled-pork barbecue."

"What's going on?" Porter strolled over to the fridge. "Who drank all the juice?" He swished the half inch of orange liquid in the plastic container.

"Sorry," Dixie said. "I gave up soda until after the baby's born."

Merle joined his siblings in the kitchen. "Are you going to breast-feed?"

The kitchen was becoming much too crowded. "I don't know. I hadn't thought that far ahead." Besides, this wasn't a conversation sisters had with brothers.

"If you breast-feed, you can't eat junk food." Merle grabbed several slices of white bread to go with his morning coffee. "You have to eat healthy stuff."

"Since when have you become an expert on lactating women's diets?" she asked as Merle dunked a piece of bread in his coffee, then shoved the sopping mess into his mouth and grinned.

"When do you have time to shop for a wedding dress?" Conway asked.

"I plan to wear Grandma's." The plain, unadorned silk had aged to a beautiful ivory color and was lovingly packed in a box beneath her bed.

"What about bridesmaids?" Conway said. "Gavin'll have groomsmen plus a best man."

"Who's Gavin gonna pick for a best man?" Merle asked.

Conway scribbled a note on the pad of paper in front of him. "I bet he picks Johnny."

"Who's picking Johnny for what?" Willie joined his siblings.

"Best man," Porter answered.

"Hold on everyone." Dixie scooted her chair back and stood. "Gavin and I aren't having a big wedding. Johnny will give me away but no bridesmaids or groomsmen."

"Why's everyone in the kitchen?" Buck came in from the wash porch.

Porter, Conway, Willie and Merle pointed at Dixie. "We're trying to plan a wedding but she's putting up a stink," Conway said.

"It's *my* wedding. I can put up a stink if I want to."

"Cold feet?" Buck's quiet voice silenced her brothers.

"No." *Maybe.* "Conway thinks I need a fancy-schmancy wedding and I want to keep things simple." She didn't dare tell her brothers that one of the reasons she didn't care for an extravagant affair was because she didn't want Gavin believing she was head-over-heels about him—just in case things didn't work out and they parted ways after the baby was born.

Her brothers' gazes swung to Buck, waiting for his response. "Dixie's the bride. She has the final say."

"Thank you, Buck. You're my favorite brother." She placed her juice glass in the sink. "Now, if you'll excuse me, I have a business to run." She stepped outside and took a deep breath, filling her lungs with cool morning air. She loved the month of October—daytime highs in the eighties and nighttime lows in the sixties—perfect sleeping weather. October made suffering through the unbearable heat of Arizona summers worthwhile. As soon as she got in her truck and cranked the engine she flipped on the radio, hoping the noise would block out her concerns over marrying Gavin.

No such luck.

Gavin's arguments in favor of marrying were sound—she was all in favor of him being involved in their child's life, but recognized from her mother's experience that a man and woman living together for the sake of a child always led to a breakup. Dixie didn't want to suffer the same heartache and bouts of depression her mother had endured as a result of failed relationships.

Then don't let Gavin steal your heart.

Too late. After all he'd done for her, there was no way Dixie could not love the man—at least a little.

Feel appreciation and gratitude, but stop there.

No can do. Their lovemaking had touched her deeply and convinced her that Gavin cared about her—how much, time would tell. The one thing that saved her from a panic attack was the knowledge that if Gavin tired of her or decided he wanted out of the marriage, she retained the gift shop in Yuma. As long as she had a means of supporting herself and the baby she'd survive without Gavin.

Dixie's cell rang. Keeping one eye on the road she

stuck her hand into her purse and rummaged through the contents until her fingers bumped the phone.

"Hello."

"It's me."

Her heart stuttered at the sound of Gavin's sexy voice. "Everything okay?"

"Yep. Just calling to see how things are going with you."

"Fine." Dixie smiled. "Where are you?"

"Chula Vista."

"You're rodeoing there?"

"No. Passing through. I'll be in San Dimas this weekend."

Because she was content working in her store each day, it didn't bother Dixie a bit that Gavin would spend the week traveling through California.

"I might look up a few army buddies while I'm out here." He cleared his throat. "How are the wedding plans going?"

"Fine."

Silence followed by, "Let me know if you need any money."

Gavin had already done more than enough and Dixie would not ask him to help pay for a wedding. "My brothers want to know if you'll be picking a best man." Dixie winced as soon as she asked the question. She hadn't meant to remind Gavin of the loss of his best friend.

"I don't have anyone in mind for a best man."

"That's fine because I'm not having a maid of honor." Shannon was the only friend she'd consider asking and Shannon was in Florida for who knew how long.

"Dixie, you don't have to—"

"No, it's all right, Gavin."

"I've got to go. Traffic is a nightmare."

"Okay. And, Gavin...thank you—" she swallowed the lump in her throat that formed when she thought of his generosity "—for buying the shop."

"Talk to you later."

The call cut off and Dixie felt a keen sense of loss. She slowed down as she drove through Stagecoach and shifted her thoughts to the gift shop and brainstorming ideas to increase sales and publicity.

"WHERE THE HELL HAVE you been, Tucker?"

Gavin grinned in the cowboy ready area at the San Dimas Western Days Rodeo in San Dimas, California. "What's the matter, Murray, afraid I'll win?"

Fellow bareback rider Ryan Murray snorted. "Army man, I can beat you with both hands tied behind my back."

Gavin shook hands with Murray—the wiry cowboy reminded him of Nate—always teasing people. "I had business to take care of in Arizona." Gavin dropped his gear bag.

"Thought maybe you had an epiphany and realized you weren't a bona fide bareback rider."

A group of competitors nearby chuckled and tipped their hats to Gavin. He'd missed sparring with the guys when he'd taken a break from the circuit to help Dixie with the store. "Why've you been hanging out in Arizona?" A cowboy named Pete Santali invited himself into the conversation. Santali was a bull rider who'd joined the circuit right out of high school and had yet to finish higher than tenth in a rodeo.

"You recall the Canyon City Rodeo in Arizona this past July?" Gavin spoke to the men.

"Sure. I rode Caramel Delight and he kicked my butt into the stands," Santali said.

"Remember the female bull riding event?"

"Hell, yes! Prettiest dang girls I ever seen ride bulls." Murray spit tobacco juice at the ground. "You hook up with one of them beauties?"

"As a matter of fact, I did. I'm engaged to Dixie Cash."

Murray whistled between his teeth. "Man, are you crazy? I sure as hell wouldn't want the Cash cowboys as brothers-in-law."

"They're not so bad." Gavin took comfort in knowing that while he was on the road, the brothers would be there to help Dixie if she needed anything.

"You gonna keep rodeoing after you marry?" Santali asked.

"Not sure." The past week he'd enjoyed being by Dixie's side and as far as small towns went, Stagecoach wasn't bad. Commuting into Yuma for a job wouldn't bother him—not if Dixie worked in her gift shop. He liked the idea of meeting her for lunch or dropping into the store to check on her and the baby during the day.

"When's the wedding?" Santali asked. "We invited?"

"Nope. We're having a family-only ceremony next month."

"You gonna look for a real job?" Murray asked.

"Eventually."

Santali chuckled. "Hell, I wouldn't know where to apply if I had to get a real job."

"I've got experience with water reclamation projects," Gavin said. "I'm hoping to find work with the city of Yuma."

"Good luck to you, man." Murray shook Gavin's

hand and Santali did the same, and then the cowboys walked off.

Gavin approached chute eight and studied his draw—a horse named Tiny Dancer—when the gelding bucked, he gave the illusion of walking on air. The horse had a fifty-fifty win streak going so Gavin had a shot of making it to eight. He rummaged through his gear bag and removed his rope and glove. The announcer droned on about the winners of the bareback event from the previous year's rodeo. Gavin appreciated that the announcer attempted to make the event sound important or relevant to the current rodeo standings, but the truth was the cowboys riding today weren't good enough to compete for the bigger purses. The Western Days rodeo was comprised of young hotheads trying to gain experience, old has-beens who refused to hang up their ropes and Gavin—guys whose lives were in limbo.

"Next up is Gavin Tucker! He's riding Tiny Dancer!"

Gavin stuffed his hand into his riding glove, then climbed the chute rails and settled on the gelding's back. He played with his grip on the rope handle, trying not to overthink his ride. He'd gotten caught up in attempting to predict a horse's moves before the chute door opened and the horse never performed as expected—most of the time Gavin sailed through the air after a few bucks.

One more twist of the rope and he nodded to the gateman. Tiny Dancer vaulted into the arena. Gavin rode out the first three bucks in succession and then the gelding got serious and added a spin to his repertoire of moves. Gavin—cocky from three seconds of success—sailed over the horse's head. He landed on the ground, skidding across the dirt on his stomach then came to a stop in a tangle of arms and legs. The fans' lukewarm applause embarrassed him as he crawled to his knees and retrieved his hat.

"Tucker," Santali hollered when Gavin stepped behind the chutes. "Hope you make a better husband than you do a rodeo cowboy."

So did Gavin.

Chapter Twelve

"Dixie, I've got to have another bar of that romance soap you sold me last week." Mildred Hinkle marched through the gift shop and stopped in front of the counter where Dixie rang up a customer. "You'll want another bar of that one." Mildred pointed to the pink-wrapped soap among the woman's purchases. "Use it to wash your delicates and I guarantee your husband will notice."

The customer nodded and Dixie added another bar from the romance collection. "That will be twenty-eight dollars and thirty-six cents." She ran the woman's credit card through the machine, then handed her a receipt to sign. "The bottom one is yours."

"Thank you for the recommendation." The woman smiled at Mrs. Hinkle.

"Happy to help."

If Dixie didn't know better, she'd swear sourpuss Mildred had become Ms. Congeniality. Left alone with the old woman she said, "I'm glad your husband approves of the soap."

"He more than approves." Mildred winked. "He came to bed before the ten o' clock news before every night this week. Hasn't done that in seventeen years."

Dixie swallowed a chuckle. "I'm working on a new

Thanksgiving soap—citrus spice." She motioned for Mildred to follow her into the kitchen at the back of the store. Each night Dixie stayed late to make soap after the shop closed—better to keep busy than sit at home and think of Gavin. She expected to miss him, but hadn't anticipated her every other thought to focus on him... What was he doing? Who was he with? Was he thinking of her?

Gavin had made a habit of phoning Dixie in the evenings to wish her good-night. He had no idea that when she answered his calls she was on the road driving back to Stagecoach. She didn't tell him she'd worked late, knowing he'd disapprove of her driving home alone at night. Or he'd insist she wasn't getting enough rest. Dixie had agreed to a wedding—not to having Gavin dictate her every move.

Mildred studied the bowls of spices and herbs on the kitchen table while Dixie fetched the sample soap and waved it beneath Mildred's nose.

"Lovely...almost good enough to eat. Is that nutmeg?"

"Yes." Dixie held up a leaf and a pumpkin-shaped mold. "Which one do you prefer?"

"Both. Have you thought of adding additional shapes like gourds and Indian corn? A bowl of harvest-scented soaps would make a terrific holiday display."

"That's a great idea. Thank you, Mrs. Hinkle."

Mildred glanced at the wall clock. "I'd better return to my store."

Dixie followed her to the front door, happy to see another customer come into the shop. She hoped the steady stream of clientele this week foreshadowed the upcoming holiday spending habits of the locals and tourists.

"Where's that handsome young man who helped you during your grand opening?"

"Gavin's rodeoing."

Mildred's gaze narrowed. "Oh, he's one of those cowboys?" She waggled a finger in front of Dixie's face. "You best keep an eye on him, dear." She leaned closer. "I know from experience that traveling men stray."

Dixie watched Mildred cross the street and walk up the block to her store. She considered the older woman's words, then discarded them. Gavin wasn't the kind of man to stray. She honestly believed when he'd proposed to her—yes, for the sake of the baby—that he planned to honor their marriage vows. Honorable intentions aside, there was the chance that after the baby was born and they set up house and established a routine that their relationship might hit a bump in the road.

There was no guarantee she and Gavin and the baby would remain a family forever, but she had to try—for the baby's sake *and* her sake. She'd rather live with the stigma of a divorce than hear gossip about her being an unwed mother. A tramp. Or worse—that she'd followed in her mother's footsteps.

"Let me know if I can answer any questions." Dixie smiled at her customer.

"I'm just browsing, thank you."

A dull twinge spread through Dixie's stomach— the third one in as many hours. She pressed her fingers against her side and returned to the kitchen. She shouldn't have eaten the pickle that came with the tuna sandwich she'd ordered from the deli.

"GAVIN! WHAT ARE YOU doing here?" Gavin's mother hugged the life out of him while he stood on the welcome mat outside her apartment.

"Miss me?" Gavin teased.

"Of course." She tugged him inside and shut the door. A baritone woof greeted him.

"Hey, Barney."

"Barney's disappointed you're not Ricardo asking us to join him and Chica on a walk."

"So it's like that between you and Ricardo?" Gavin tossed his Stetson on top of his mother's coffee table, removed his phone from his pocket and turned off the ringer before sitting on the couch next to the old bulldog. He scratched Barney behind the ears.

"Ricardo and I are friends. Nothing more." His mother retrieved a can of Gavin's favorite cola from the fridge.

"What's the expiration date on this?"

"Ha-ha. Maybe you should visit your mother more often." She patted his cheek. "I'll make you a sandwich—"

"No thanks, Mom. I ate on the way into town."

His mother returned to her recliner. "Why didn't you tell me you were coming to Phoenix? I would have asked for time off from work."

"I can't stay. I'm on my way to Winslow."

"Another rodeo?"

"Yep."

"Looks like you've been staying healthy unless you're hiding a cast under that shirt."

"No broken bones. Sore muscles and achy joints but that's nothing new."

"How's Dixie?"

"Good."

"Just good?"

"We set a wedding date."

"Then things between you two are better than good."

His mother smiled. "Have you decided where you'll live after you marry?"

Gavin read between the lines of his mother's question. She wanted him to settle near her in Phoenix. "A lot has happened since we last talked."

"And whose fault is that? You only phone every two weeks."

"I'll try to do better." Gavin smiled sheepishly. After years in the military where he'd been in the habit of phoning home once a month he had trouble keeping track of the time between calls to his mother.

Yet you remembered to check in with Dixie every night this past week.

"Dixie and I bought a gift shop in Yuma and she's selling her homemade soaps there." His mother would only worry if she discovered Gavin had taken out the loan but the store belonged to Dixie.

"Does this mean you're going to retire from rodeo?"

"Not yet. Perfumed soaps aren't my thing. Dixie's in charge of the store."

"How long do you plan to rodeo, then?"

Gavin sympathized with his mother worrying over his health and safety. She'd spent six years fretting about him in the army. He'd come back alive from a war zone and she still had to worry he'd get his head stomped in by a bronc. "I'll rodeo until the baby's born."

"And Dixie's due date is...?"

"Sometime in March. I'm planning to look for a civilian job after Christmas. Hopefully I'll find work in Yuma."

"So you and Dixie intend to stay in Yuma?"

"No. Dixie's lived her entire life in Stagecoach, Mom. The family farm means a lot to her and they lease the pecan groves to a business corporation so she'll want to be close by to keep an eye on things." Her six brothers could do the eye-keeping, but in truth, Stagecoach had grown on Gavin.

When he'd left the army he'd planned to live in a big city where he could go about his daily routine with a good amount of anonymity. With a baby on the way and he and Dixie marrying, Gavin believed the best environment for their child was among friends and family.

"Would you consider moving to Yuma? It's not that far from Stagecoach." It had always been the two of them—Gavin's grandparents had disowned his mother when she'd turned up pregnant.

"Is that your roundabout way of asking if I'll take care of the baby while you and Dixie work?"

"Not at all. Dixie's going to bring the baby to the shop with her."

If push came to shove, Gavin would admit fatherhood was scarier than fighting the Taliban and he'd appreciate having his mother's support and guidance.

"I'd like nothing better than to live closer to you and the baby, but I love my job with the parks department and Ricardo..." Her cheeks turned pink.

His mother had never dated while she'd raised him—at least not to Gavin's knowledge. "You love this man?"

"Not love. I like Ricardo very much. He's a widower and we enjoy each other's company."

"No pressure, Mom. I want you to be happy. Just know you can visit Dixie and me as often as you want."

"I will do that. Are you planning to live at her farm, then?"

Gavin cringed at the prospect of sharing a house with the Cash brothers. "For a while, I guess."

"What's the matter, honey? You seem—" his mother waved a hand in the air by her face "—unsettled."

Needing to voice his fear out loud, he said, "I'm not sure Dixie's as committed to making our marriage work as I am."

"Go on."

"Dixie and I have gone about this whole thing in an unconventional way." He ran his fingers through his hair. "She didn't tell me she was pregnant. I had to confront her. In the beginning I wasn't ready for marriage and only wanted to offer financial support." Gavin popped off the couch and paced by the front door. "Then I had a change of heart."

Because being with Dixie makes you feel good inside.

"I insisted that Dixie and I marry for the baby's sake."

His mother's eyes widened.

"I know it sounds bad, but Dixie grew up without a father, too, and I thought she'd appreciate my gesture."

"I'm guessing she didn't."

"No. She rejected my proposal and…"

"And what?"

"I was relieved."

"Why?"

"I wasn't ready to settle down, Mom. I've been on the move with the army for so long I didn't think I could stay in one place and be happy." Gavin's explanation was weak at best.

"Then Dixie and I spent more time together and got to know each other better. So I thought, why not do what was best for the baby and maybe along the way we'd all become a real family."

"Dixie didn't see things your way?"

"No. She agreed to an engagement but wanted to wait to marry until after the baby was born."

"What changed her mind about setting a wedding date?"

That was the million-dollar question. "I don't know." He didn't want to believe Dixie felt indebted to him for buying the shop in Yuma. Or that after making love in the shower she'd allowed her hormones to speak for her. Gavin hoped her feelings for him were deepening.

"Have either of you said the words *I love you?*"

Gavin dropped his gaze to the tips of his boots. "No."

"Then maybe the wedding should wait."

Dixie was skittish enough about marrying. If Gavin suddenly got cold feet and suggested they postpone their nuptials he'd never convince her to pick another date. "I think it's best we marry now not after the baby's born."

"All right. You can count on me to be at the wedding."

"Thanks."

"And, honey, I'm always here for you if you need to talk."

Gavin hugged his mother. "I know."

"I hope Dixie appreciates your integrity and all you're willing to do for her."

"She does." Appreciation wasn't the problem, but convincing Dixie to commit a hundred percent to their marriage was an obstacle he'd yet to overcome. Being away from Dixie this week had taught Gavin how much he needed her. With Dixie by his side, he could defeat the enemies who stalked him at night. Without Dixie… Gavin feared the worst—a life on the run and no relationship with his own child.

"JOHNNY," DIXIE GASPED.

"Hey, sis, what's up?"

Another sharp pain stabbed Dixie in the side and she broke out in a cold sweat. "Are you busy?"

"I'm on my way into Yuma to pick up a new pair of jeans. The back pocket ripped the other day and—"

"Meet me at the Yuma Regional Medical Center."

"What happened?"

She gripped the clipboard in her hand until another pain passed. "It's the baby." Finished filling out the medical forms, Dixie stood. As soon as she took a step, a rush of warmth spread between her legs. Horrified, she glanced down. A dark stain spread across the crotch of her jeans. Feeling faint, she collapsed on the chair and the phone dropped into her lap.

The redheaded nurse behind the station desk summed up the situation and called for a wheelchair. An orderly appeared and they helped Dixie into the chair, then wheeled her into a curtained-off cubicle where the nurse assisted her in putting on a hospital gown. When Dixie caught sight of her bloody underwear tears filled her eyes.

"Hang on, dear." The nurse helped her onto the hospital bed and stuffed a pad between her legs before picking up the phone and calling for a doctor. The nurse returned to Dixie's side and took her vital signs. "How far along are you?"

"Fourteen weeks."

The nurse patted Dixie's hand. "The doctor will be here soon."

"Am I losing the baby?"

"I don't know, but we'll do everything we can to help you."

Left alone in the sterile room Dixie closed her eyes and prayed for her baby.

A few minutes later a middle-age man flung the curtain aside and stepped into the cubical. "I'm Dr. Davidson." He scanned Dixie's medical chart. "Did you fall or hurt yourself today?"

"No." She hadn't fallen. Hadn't bumped into anything. "I began feeling sharp twinges this morning and they became worse after lunch."

"What have you eaten today?"

"Toast, orange juice. A pickle and a tuna sandwich."

"Let's take a look at you." The nurse rolled an ultrasound machine next to the bed and the doctor squirted cold jelly across Dixie's stomach. She gave him credit for maintaining a poker face. The nurse watching the monitor wasn't a good actress—she wouldn't make eye contact with Dixie.

I'm losing the baby.

"I'm sorry. The placenta tore away from the uterine wall and the baby no longer has a heartbeat." He squeezed Dixie's arm gently. "Sometimes these things happen and there's no explanation why." He scribbled on the medical chart then asked, "This was your first pregnancy?"

Dixie nodded, still struggling to process the news that she'd lost the baby.

"You'll be able to try for another baby as soon as your body has had time to heal."

I won't be able to try again—not with Gavin. Her throat thickened and she struggled to catch her breath.

"I'll need to perform a D and C once you expel the fetus." He looked at the nurse. "Call me when she's ready."

As soon as the doctor left the room the nurse started an IV and a few minutes later, Dixie felt contractions. Offering words of encouragement and sympathy, the nurse held her hand and it was over in twenty minutes.

After administering a sedative, the doctor performed a D and C. Dixie had no idea how much time had passed when he peeled off his gloves, patted her shoulder and told her to follow up with her gynecologist as soon as possible. Then he was gone.

"Would you like to see your daughter?" the nurse whispered as if the baby were sleeping and not dead.

My daughter?

The nurse held a towel between her hands, and there in the middle of the cloth lay a teeny-tiny baby approximately four inches long. The most beautiful little being Dixie had ever seen.

"You can hold her," the nurse said.

Tears blurred her vision as Dixie cradled the towel in her lap. Gently she brushed the tip of a finger over her daughter's head. *I love you, sweetheart. I'm so sorry. So sorry. Your daddy loves you, too.* Dixie pressed the pad of her index finger against her daughter's lifeless heart. *Find Grandma Ada, sweetie. She'll take care of you in Heaven and one day we'll be together again.* Dixie pressed a kiss to the baby's face, then handed her back to the nurse.

"Have you picked a name?" The nurse's eyes shone with unshed tears.

"Adelle. Addy for short. After her great-grandmother."

"It's a beautiful name." The nurse gently placed the towel on the instrument tray. "We have a chaplain on duty."

Dixie shook her head no.

"Would you prefer the hospital make arrangements for the baby or did you—"

"She's going home with me." Dixie would bury little Addy in the family plot next to her great-grandmother.

"Who should we call for you while you're recovering?"

"My brother's on his way."

"Try to rest. Once the bleeding slows down and you feel well enough to stand and walk, you'll be released. When your brother arrives I'll send him in to sit with you."

"Thank you."

"I'm sorry you lost your little girl." The nurse slid the curtain closed, allowing Dixie privacy to mourn.

Alone at last, tears leaked from her eyes, dribbled down her temples and pooled in her ears.

Gavin, where are you? I need you.

Dixie cried herself to sleep. When she woke all six of her brothers stood by her bedside. They might be the most bothersome, demanding, opinionated, bossy brothers a girl could have but they'd dropped whatever they'd been doing and had rushed to her side.

Johnny leaned down and hugged her. "I'm sorry, Dix."

Throat aching she glanced at each brother through watery eyes. "Did the nurse tell you?"

"Tell us what?" Merle asked.

"The baby was a girl."

Johnny cleared his throat. "She told us you wanted to take her home to bury her."

"If we had a girl, Gavin and I had decided to name her Adelle. I want to bury her next to Grandma Ada."

"That's a good idea," Porter said. "Grandma would be real honored you picked her name."

"Have you told Gavin?" Conway asked.

Dixie shook her head. "I called a couple of times but his phone went straight to voice mail. I didn't leave a message." It didn't seem right to tell Gavin she'd lost their baby in a voice message.

"We'll track him down," Johnny said.

She squeezed Johnny's fingers. "Tell Gavin that I don't want to see him." What was the point? There was no baby so there would be no marriage.

"What about the wedding?" Merle asked.

"There isn't going to be one."

Her brothers frowned.

"What do you mean there won't be a wedding?" Conway asked.

"Gavin's off the hook." Dixie grimaced at the sight of her soiled clothes resting on the chair. "I can't wear my jeans."

"The nurse left a pair of scrubs for you." Johnny pointed to the outfit at the foot of the bed.

"Give me some privacy to dress. I want to go—" her voice broke "—home." Dixie wished her grandmother waited for her at the farm—Grandma Ada always knew how to heal a hurting heart.

Chapter Thirteen

"Why the hell haven't you been answering your cell, Tucker?"

Gavin held the phone away from his ear. The irate caller sounded like Dixie's brother. "Johnny?"

"I've been trying to get ahold of you since Monday."

"Sorry. My phone's been turning off on its own. I need a new—"

"Never mind your phone. It's Dixie."

Fear shot through Gavin, leaving him cold. He'd left a voice mail on Dixie's cell after the rodeo in Winslow on Sunday but she'd never returned his call. Figuring she'd been busy with the store or she'd gotten tired of him phoning, he'd backed off and hadn't attempted to contact her the past two days. He wanted to surprise her and show up in person at the gift shop tomorrow. "What's wrong, Johnny? Is she okay?"

"Dixie's…fine. Get here as soon as you can."

Gavin checked his mirrors, then pulled over to the side of the road and waited for three vehicles to pass. Coast clear, he made a U-turn and headed west on I-8. "I'm three hours away."

"Drive safe." *Click.*

Whatever was going on with Dixie must be serious if Johnny wouldn't say over the phone.

Don't jump to conclusions.

Maybe there'd been trouble at the gift shop. Had the place been robbed or vandalized? Or had Dixie changed her mind about the wedding—again. Was she back to wanting to marry after the baby's birth in March or worse...wanted to cancel the wedding altogether.

What if it's the baby?

As soon as the thought entered his mind, Gavin rejected it. Worrying wouldn't get him to the farm any faster. He put the pedal to the metal and pushed the truck to eighty. He could afford a ticket on his untarnished driving record. Hoping to keep his thoughts from straying to Dixie he turned on the radio and listened to a sports talk show.

Gavin cruised through Stagecoach at 10:15 p.m. His stomach growled, but he ignored the hunger pangs as he zipped through town, which was dead on a Wednesday night. Only the bars remained open, their neon beer signs glowing in the windows.

Tonight the Arizona sky was darker than usual—not even the silhouette of the Gila Mountains was visible to the southwest. He slowed the truck as he approached the turnoff to the farm. When he pulled up to the farmhouse, lights blazed from the windows on both floors and the Cash brothers' pickups were scattered about the yard. Gavin parked behind Merle's truck and hurried to the house, taking the porch steps two at a time. He didn't bother knocking. When he stepped into the kitchen he found Dixie's siblings playing cards, Halloween candy substituting for poker chips.

Six somber faces stared at Gavin. He got the chills all over again.

Johnny stood. "Let's talk in the living room."

Gavin followed Dixie's eldest brother down the hall and Johnny shut the French doors behind them.

"Where's Dixie?" Gavin asked.

"Upstairs sleeping. I'd wake her but she's had a rough time of it and needs her sleep." The dull sheen in Johnny's blue eyes socked Gavin in the gut.

"Why hasn't Dixie been sleeping?"

"Look, Gavin. I shouldn't be the one telling you this, but if it were left up to Dixie who knows when you'd find out."

"Find out what?"

"She lost the baby on Monday."

The blood drained from Gavin's head and he sank onto the sofa. He hadn't wanted to believe something had happened to the baby but his instincts had been right all along. "Is Dixie okay?"

"Physically...yes. Emotionally she's a wreck."

Dixie taking the loss of their baby hard comforted Gavin in an odd way. They hadn't planned this pregnancy. Neither of them had been ready for parenthood, yet Dixie mourned for their child despite the fact that she was suddenly free of any long-term obligation. His chest felt numb...his hands cold. "How did she lose the baby?" He envisioned Dixie tumbling off a stepladder at the shop or tripping on the sidewalk.

"The doctor said sometimes these things happen and there's no real explanation why."

"She's been working too hard." He'd gone off to rodeo and left Dixie to handle the shop on her own. "I should have stayed and—"

"Don't blame yourself, Gavin. It wasn't your fault or Dixie's. It just happened." Johnny cleared his throat. "I'm sure you'll want to see her in the morning."

Did Dixie want to see him?

"I'll scrounge up an extra blanket and pillow. You can sleep on the couch." Johnny paused at the door. "And, Gavin?"

"What?"

"Keep things light between you and Dixie in the morning. She needs cheering up."

DIXIE WOKE TO THE SUN shining through her bedroom window. She squinted at the bright light. There was nothing *sunny* about the day ahead. She shifted on the mattress, the dull ache inside her still present. Her eyes misted. She'd cried so hard and so long Monday night after she'd returned from the hospital that there weren't any tears left inside her…just mist.

Her gaze fixated on the jewelry box her grandmother gave her. If she focused on an inanimate object long enough maybe she'd find the strength to dress for the day. She couldn't afford to spend another twenty-four hours in bed dwelling on the baby. She had to keep busy. Occupy her mind with other things. After breakfast she'd drive into Yuma and open the shop.

She swung her legs off the side of the mattress and sat up. She breathed deeply then grimaced. She needed a shower and her hair needed a shampoo. As if removed from her body, she shuffled across the room and rummaged through the dresser drawer. Clean clothes in hand she padded down the hall, noticing her brothers' bedroom doors stood open. Hopefully they'd left for the day—she wanted the house to herself.

The warm shower felt wonderful and Dixie stood beneath the pulsing water until it cooled. After drying off she smoothed lotion on her body and brushed her teeth. Once she blew her hair dry, she secured the long strands in a ponytail and went downstairs. She froze in the hallway.

Gavin. Asleep on the living room couch, his sock feet hanging over the edge.

Her eyes misted. Again.

Damn her brothers for interfering. She'd insisted she'd tell Gavin about the baby when she was ready. She was *not* ready right now. She fled to the kitchen where she found a note on the fridge, held in place by a saguaro magnet.

Porter and Buck opened the gift shop today. The rest of us are heading over to the Johnsons' to put a new roof on their barn. Call if you need anything. Johnny.

More mist in her eyes. Maybe by the end of the day she'd produce enough moisture to form a teardrop.

Dixie removed the carton of orange juice from the fridge, then promptly returned it to the shelf and shut the door. Her reason for eating healthy was…gone. She started a pot of coffee and gazed out the window above the sink. She had no idea how to handle things between her and Gavin.

Now that there was no baby she couldn't expect Gavin to keep paying the mortgage on the gift shop and she couldn't afford to buy him out. She supposed they'd have to put the place up for sale. Dixie didn't know how long she gazed out the window before Gavin's image materialized in the sparkling glass. Bracing herself, she faced him.

He looked tired and rumpled after a night on the couch. Their gazes locked. Neither moved. Neither spoke. The air thickened and silence echoed through the room in thunderous waves. Just when she feared she'd pass out from holding her breath, Gavin moved across the room and pulled her close, his hug firm.

Dixie's defenses were at an all-time low and she had no willpower to resist Gavin. In fact she desperately welcomed his sympathy. She could have stood in his arms forever—warm, safe and protected from reality. But touching Gavin…absorbing his comfort…breathing his scent…would only make the goodbye more difficult.

Slowly, as if her arms were lead pipes instead of flesh and bone, she released her hold and attempted to pull away.

Gavin held her prisoner, tightening his hold. Then he did the unthinkable—he kissed the top of her head, the gesture weakening her defenses.

Hadn't she bawled enough since Monday? She collapsed against Gavin, her tears soaking the front of his shirt.

He caressed her shoulders, uttered meaningless phrases in her ear and kissed her neck, his rough whiskers pricking her jaw. She cried forever—until the rumble of his deep voice filtered into her ear.

"What?" she choked out.

"Coffee's done."

She slipped from his embrace, wiped her eyes on a dish towel and poured two mugs of coffee. They sat across from each other at the table, Gavin's face sober. Sad. Concerned. Self-consciously she touched her cheeks. Three days of sobbing had left her with puffy eyes and blotchy skin. "What time did you get here last night?"

"After you'd already gone to bed." He frowned. "If you called me, I'm sorry. My phone's been turning off on its own. I need to upgrade to a new model."

She'd attempted to contact Gavin from the hospital before she'd lost the baby. Afterward, she hadn't had the courage to tell him. "Are you hungry?"

He shook his head.

Dixie hated beating around the bush. "Did Johnny tell you?"

"I'm sorry, Dixie."

She watched for a sign of how deeply the loss of their baby affected him, but his face remained expressionless. Playing the *tough guy* came naturally to a man who'd been in the army.

"How are things at the shop?" he asked.

Startled by the change in subject, it took Dixie a moment to formulate a response. "Fine."

"Christmas will be here soon," he said. "Are you going to run any specials?" He grinned. "Two-for-one deals?"

"I haven't thought that far ahead." That he didn't ask questions about the baby hurt. He must be relieved to be free of the responsibility of fatherhood.

"Do you ski?" he asked.

Why were they talking about skiing? "I went skiing once with Shannon. I sprained my knee and never tried it again."

"I might head up to the White Mountains this winter and take a few lessons."

Gavin rose from his chair and took his mug to the sink. "It's a beautiful day. You feel like taking a drive and grabbing breakfast out?"

Sunshine didn't equate to a beautiful day. And no, she didn't feel up to a drive. "I'm not in the mood, thanks."

"There's a rodeo in Goodyear next weekend."

That Gavin kept bringing up the future pointed to

the obvious—he didn't view himself as tied down any-more. He was off the hook for being a father and a hus-band. So why all the chitchat? Why didn't Gavin come right out and say he intended to hit the road for good?

He's too honorable. Gavin was principled to the core and would not end their engagement or call off the wed-ding, because he was a man of his word and when he made a promise or a pledge he saw it through. He'd wait for Dixie to sever their relationship.

"You could come to the rodeo in Goodyear if one of your brothers will watch the gift shop."

"Gavin, stop." Ignoring his startled stare she said, "You don't have to do this."

"Do what?"

"Pretend nothing has changed between us."

"I'm not following."

Dixie had lost Gavin—a man who'd turned out to be more than she'd ever dreamed of. "There's no baby so there's no need for a wedding."

He remained silent—more proof in Dixie's mind that calling off the wedding was exactly what he'd hoped she'd do.

"We don't need to make any decisions right away," he said.

Darn him for pretending to care. "I'll try my best to cover the mortgage payments on the shop."

"The shop was a gift. As far as the monthly mort-gage I'm more than happy—"

"No."

He studied her for a long while, but Dixie wouldn't back down. Nor would she take charity. *Then why did you accept the gift shop in the first place?* She'd done it for the baby—not herself.

"I'll finish the repairs to the store that I didn't get to before the grand opening."

"Thanks, but my brothers can handle a few minor fix-it problems."

Gavin cleared his throat. "Then I guess there's no reason to stay."

Dixie wanted to scream, "Stay for me. For us." The words stuck to the sides of her throat. "You're free to go."

The stillness in the room suffocated her and she feared she'd pass out. Gavin inched toward the door. "See you…"

She hoped not. The nicest thing Gavin could do for her was remain as far away as possible. Running into him would remind her of what she'd almost had—a baby…a husband…a family of her own.

She felt compelled to speak as she followed him to the door. "Good luck with your rodeo career." Now that she was no longer his obligation, Gavin could concentrate on his bareback riding.

"If you need anything…call."

"Thanks, but I won't…" *Need you.*

Hand on the knob he glanced over his shoulder and Dixie yearned to kiss him one more time. *Don't you dare.* If she kissed Gavin she'd never have the courage to kick him out of her life. She'd resort to every female trick in the book to keep him by her side.

The only way to end this torture was to part ways. "Safe travels, Gavin." After the door shut, she peeked out the window and watched him walk to his truck. He paused, fingers on the door handle, as he studied the ground for the longest time.

Go, Gavin. Get in the truck and leave. Please don't make this any harder than it already is.

Dixie spun away. Leaning her back against the wall, she lowered herself until her rump hit the floor. Drawing her knees to her chest she buried her face in her hands. The rumble of Gavin's truck engine echoed outside. Then blessed silence.

There. It was done. Over. Finished.

Dixie was back to being alone again.

GAVIN LEFT STAGECOACH and drove with no particular destination in mind, afraid if he stopped, he'd think. He didn't want to reflect on Dixie losing the baby. Him losing Dixie. His survival instincts kicked in and a numbness settled deep in his bones, protecting him from the pain. He drove for hours, stopping for gas and food once.

Fatigue and hunger compelled him to pull into a Love's Travel Plaza at 10:00 p.m. *Where the hell am I?* He must have passed a dozen highway signs yet he hadn't read any of them. He parked next to a car with a New Mexico license plate and got out. He winced as a muscle spasm gripped his calf when he took his first step. He limped on, his wobbly gait drawing stares from an older couple leaving the building. Inside the truck stop he noticed a banner above the entrance to the convenience store—Welcome to Albuquerque.

After using the bathroom Gavin sat at a table in the adjoining restaurant and flipped over the white mug. A waitress named Heather filled the cup with coffee and left a menu. "Be back in a jiffy."

Gavin perused his options until the waitress returned. "What can I get you?" she asked.

"Are there any specials?"

"Sorry." Heather shook her head, her blond curls

bouncing against her face. "Mac—" she nodded toward the kitchen "—cooks a mean breakfast."

Gavin skimmed the breakfast items. "I'll take the Number 1 with wheat toast and sausage instead of bacon."

"Sure thing." Heather placed silverware on the table then hurried off.

Gavin sat in a stupor, sipping his coffee. A baby's shrill cry interrupted his trance. A woman toting an infant carrier walked through the dining area and picked a table in the middle of the room—right in Gavin's line of vision. He was powerless to look away as the young mother placed the carrier on a chair and removed the baby. She pressed her lips to the top of the infant's fuzzy head and the baby's cries softened to a whimper.

The numbness that had protected Gavin from his thoughts slowly melted and a burning tingle spread through his chest as he acknowledged what he and Dixie had lost. Their baby had been real...yet not real. Shoot, Dixie hadn't begun showing before she'd lost the baby. And sadly he hadn't gone to a doctor's appointment and seen his child's image through an ultrasound nor had he felt the baby kick in Dixie's stomach.

The infant across the room was dressed from head to booties in blue—a boy. When a young man joined the woman and reached for the baby, Gavin curled his fingers into a fist. What would it have felt like to hold his child? He wished he'd asked Dixie if the baby had been a boy or girl.

A son or a daughter.

Losing their child was painful but Dixie cutting him loose was crippling. She'd been his reason...his strength to move forward with his life and put the ugliness of his past behind him. Without her by his side, Gavin feared all the progress he'd made toward burying his demons would be lost.

He guessed it didn't matter what *he* wanted because what he wanted—Dixie—didn't want him back. Gavin was left with no choice but to move on.

To what?

To the one thing he sucked at—rodeo.

Chapter Fourteen

"Thank you for stopping in." Dixie flashed a saccharine smile. As soon as the woman left the store another walked in. Keeping her smile in place she said, "Let me know if I can help you with anything."

Dixie glanced at the wall calendar behind the counter. Today was Friday, November 3. A dull ache spread through her chest. Tomorrow would have been her and Gavin's wedding. The days since he'd left Stagecoach dragged by for Dixie—probably because her every other thought drifted to Gavin.

Where was he?

Did he mourn the baby they'd lost?

Did he miss her?

The bell on the door jingled again. Mildred Hinkle. The old biddy had dropped by every day since she'd heard about Dixie's miscarriage—thanks to Johnny's big mouth. Worried about her depression her brother had asked Mildred to keep an eye on her. She appreciated that Millie—Dixie had joined the Main Street Merchants League and was now allowed to call Mrs. Hinkle by her nickname—had offered a sympathetic ear if Dixie felt like discussing her miscarriage and broken engagement. Dixie preferred to keep her feelings to herself.

"Hello, Millie. How's business at your end of the block?"

"Oh, fine, dear." After years of being a curmudgeon, Mildred had little experience cheering people up, but Dixie appreciated her efforts. Mildred motioned to the half-empty Christmas display on the counter. "Your preholiday sales are doing well."

"Sales this week have been incredibly…"

Mildred blinked. "Incredibly what, dear?"

Was Mildred behind the increase in shoppers browsing Dixie's Desert Delights the past few days? "Millie, have you been sending your customers my way?"

"I might have suggested they check out your soap selection…"

Annoyed by Mildred's confession, Dixie swallowed a sharp retort. If people didn't stop pitying her she'd never gain the strength to forget Gavin—as if that was even possible. "Thank you for the referrals, Millie, but everyone's on tight budgets these days. You can't afford to turn down sales."

"I've been in business for over twenty years and I have more loyal customers than I know what to do with."

No use arguing with the Main Street matriarch. "I think I'll close up early today," Dixie said. Pretending to be happy exhausted her.

"Good idea. You need your rest."

Dixie walked Mildred to the door.

"You're feeling better now?" Mildred asked.

A loaded question if ever there was one. "I am."

"Good. See you tomorrow."

As soon as Dixie shut the door behind Mildred she flipped the sign in the window to Closed. When she turned away she came face-to-face with a customer.

"Good grief, I'm sorry. I didn't mean to lock you inside."

"That's all right. If it's not too late, I'd like to buy these." She held out three bars of soap.

"Certainly." Dixie rang up the purchase then thanked the woman and let her out. Dixie spent an hour straightening the shop for the next day. When there was nothing more to do, she resigned herself to heading back to the farm—her *least* favorite place to be now.

The farm had once been her refuge but memories of Gavin followed her everywhere—from the barn to her bedroom to the kitchen to the pecan grove behind the house. If confronting Gavin's memory at the farm wasn't difficult enough then her brothers' attempts to cheer her up threatened to send her across the border.

Resigned to her fate, Dixie drove to Stagecoach. As she passed through town an unbearable urge for a cold beer hit her and she swung into the parking lot of Gilly's Tap House. A handful of trucks sat parked outside and none of them belonged to her brothers.

Loud music smacked Dixie upside the head when she entered the tavern. A raucous game of pool competed with the whiny sounds of a steel guitar blaring from the jukebox. An older couple, heads bent in conversation, occupied a table in the corner and two cowboys—probably local ranch hands—sat at the bar. Dixie chose a stool at the far end—she wasn't in the mood for company—especially the cowboy kind.

"Tough day at the office?" The barkeep slapped a drink napkin on the bar.

"You could say that. Coors Light, please." A frosty bottle appeared in front of her. "Keep a tab."

The bartender nodded, then meandered back to the

cowboys and launched a discussion of the most recent NASCAR race.

Dixie's first swallow of beer was refreshing.

The second sip tasted like paradise.

The third made her belch. She wiped the back of her hand across her mouth. She'd better slow down since she was drinking on an empty stomach. She kept snacks at the store but had been too busy to eat. Come to think of it, she'd skipped lunch every day this week. She hadn't gotten on the scale since… She assumed she'd lost more than the baby weight she'd gained before the miscarriage.

There she went again thinking about the baby. She chugged the beer. Before she'd finished the bottle, the barkeep placed another one in front of her and nodded to the cowboys a few stools away. Dixie glanced sideways and the men saluted her with their beers.

She smiled her thanks. While Dixie nursed her beer, she surrendered the fight to ban Gavin from her thoughts. Like a drug addict giving up cocaine, Dixie acknowledged the road ahead would be painful and filled with failed attempts to forget Gavin—but it was a path she had to travel if she intended to heal.

Dixie's thoughts drifted back in time to when she and Gavin first met. There had been something intriguing and mysterious about the soldier cowboy. She knew from the get-go that she wasn't the kind of woman men like Gavin pursued but that hadn't stopped her from chasing him.

There. She admitted it. She was to blame for the mess she was in.

The barkeep delivered a third beer. The mellow voice of Patsy Cline singing "I Fall to Pieces" echoed from the jukebox. How long would Dixie continue to fall apart until there were no pieces of her left and she hit rock bottom?

"You're not drunk, are you?"

The voice startled Dixie and she jumped inside her skin. "What are you doing here?"

"I could ask you the same question." Johnny signaled the bartender for a beer.

"Leave me alone."

"Feeling sorry for yourself?"

Dixie gasped but her outrage was cut off by a hiccup. Go figure her eldest brother would use meanness to bully her out of a funk.

Sheesh. Where was a woman to go to find a little peace if not a bar? "How'd you know I was here?"

"I was on my way into Yuma and spotted your truck in the lot."

"You should have kept going. I'm not in the mood for socializing." She guzzled the remainder of her beer and signaled for a fourth.

"How many have you had?" Johnny asked.

Not nearly enough to banish Gavin from her memory. "Bug off."

"You haven't strung two nice words together since you lost the baby."

Johnny was the only brother who wasn't afraid to say the word *baby* in front of her. The others avoided the subject because they feared any reference to the miscarriage would send their sister over the edge.

A lump formed in Dixie's throat. "I never expected things to turn out like this," she said. She had volunteered to go with Gavin to his motel room that fateful night but she honestly hadn't planned on getting pregnant.

And you never expected to fall in love with him.

"Lots of women lose babies. Yeah, it hurts but life goes on and one day you'll wake up and be pregnant again," Johnny said.

Dixie snorted. "You suck at making people feel better." She chugged her beer. "It's not just the baby."

Johnny leaned closer. "Then what is it, Dix?"

"Gavin." She rested her head against Johnny's shoulder. "I tried not to fall in love with him." All that nonsense in the beginning when she refused to marry Gavin had been a feeble attempt to avoid admitting she was falling under his spell.

"Don't confuse appreciation for Gavin buying you the gift shop with love."

"I'm not." The moment her eyes had connected with Gavin's at the Canyon City Rodeo she'd sensed his decency and time had validated her intuition. Gavin was a great guy. She recalled the nice things he'd done for her. The sacrifices he'd made for her and the baby. He'd turned out to be more than she'd ever dreamed of… hoped for…desired.

And she'd lost him.

"There will be other babies and other men," Johnny said.

"I know you mean well, but you're making me feel worse."

"You really love Gavin?"

"With all my heart."

"Then why'd you let him walk away?"

"Because he acted like he didn't care that I'd lost the baby."

"What did he say?"

"He said he was sorry about the baby and then he said it was such a nice day we should take a ride. Then he talked about skiing this winter and rodeoing. He didn't even ask me—" Dixie shook her head "—if the baby was a girl or a boy."

"Damn." Johnny hugged her. "That's my fault. I warned Gavin not to mention the baby because you were depressed."

"You're such a dumb-ass." Dixie punched his arm.

"Hey, don't blame me. Any time one of us mentioned the baby you bawled your head off."

"Doesn't matter." She wiped her runny nose on Johnny's shirt. "Now that there's no baby, there's no reason for Gavin to be with me."

"What if he loves you?"

"He doesn't." That he'd left her and Stagecoach in the dust was proof of that.

"Did you tell Gavin you love him?"

"No."

"Did you ask him if he loved you?"

She drew in a quick breath. "Of course not."

"Then I guess you don't have much choice."

Dixie squirmed out of Johnny's hold and wiped her tears away. "What do you mean?"

"Find Gavin and tell him how you feel."

What if she spilled her guts like a lovesick fool only to have her worst fear confirmed—Gavin's feelings for her had been tied to the baby and without the baby, those feelings were gone? "And if he doesn't love me?"

"Then you come home and get on with life."

And cry. Oh, Lord, would she cry.

Johnny was right. She had to find Gavin and confess her feelings for him. Only then would she know how he truly felt about her. Dixie couldn't live with herself if there was the tiniest chance he might love her. She slid off the stool and stumbled sideways, her head buzzing from too many beers.

Johnny steadied her. "Where're you going?"

"To find Gavin."

"Tomorrow's soon enough. Right now you need a good night's sleep."

Johnny escorted her out of the bar, but Dixie put the brakes on in the middle of the parking lot. "I didn't pay for my drinks."

"I took care of the tab." He guided her to his truck. "I'll have Merle and Porter fetch your pickup later. They're going barhopping tonight in Yuma."

"Johnny." Dixie crawled into the front seat. "Will you come with me to find Gavin?"

"Sorry, baby girl." Her brother hadn't used her pet name in years. "You've got to do this on your own," he said.

"What about the store?" she asked.

"Porter will watch over it. He loves talking to women."

"He'll probably sell out my inventory," Dixie muttered.

As they pulled away from the bar, Johnny pointed out the windshield at a passing van with the words Pony Express written in bold letters across the doors. "That's the new taxi service for drunk cowboys."

"What?"

Johnny grinned. "You may need that number if Gavin doesn't want you back."

"You're such a snot."

"Hey, that's what big brothers are for...making little sisters miserable."

Dixie was miserable. She shifted her gaze to the starry heavens. *Grandma, help me win Gavin back.*

YOU THINK WE CAN LEAVE the village early today?

In the far reaches of Gavin's subconscious he knew how this conversation would end and fought to ignore the strong pull of Nate's voice.

My mom sent cookies for my birthday—chocolate peanut butter. I bet they're waiting for me back at base.

Gavin struggled to open his eyes but only darkness filled his vision as if someone had placed his IBA vest over his face. The Interceptor Body Armor smelled of dust, blood, urine and sweat. He hated that stinking desert ghetto.

We got a leave coming up next month. After we visit our moms do you want to head to Texas to rodeo?

Hands and feet throbbing, Gavin opened his mouth wider but the pressure building in his chest blocked the gasps of air from reaching his lungs. His heart raced faster and faster as if the organ were held hostage on a runaway train.

Can I drive the lead Humvee back to the base? C'mon, Gavin, it's my birthday. Let me drive it.

A loud explosion was followed by a light so bright it burned Gavin's eyes and they watered. Red. Lots of red. Blood everywhere. Muted screams ringing in his ears. Soldiers running helter-skelter, calling out commands while Gavin stood immobile, the rubber soles of his boots melting into the hot desert sand.

The echo of Nate's voice propelled Gavin up the line of armored vehicles to the lead Humvee where Nate's torso lay. Gavin dropped to his knees, cradled his friend's head in his lap and looked into his lifeless eyes.

Don't touch him! Gavin waved off his comrades who approached to help. Gently he set Nate on the ground. Rage filled him—unlike anything he'd experienced since entering combat duty. He wanted to kill something—no, someone. A life for a life.

He stumbled fifty yards into the desert to collect Nate's legs. He found the left leg first, then switched directions and retrieved the right leg. He returned to the Humvee and placed the legs beneath Nate's torso where they were supposed to be. Then he turned his rage on the villagers, wielding his firearm threateningly, demanding they turn over those guilty of planting the roadside bomb.

Wait… Something wasn't right.

The scent of honeysuckle—not blood and burned flesh—drifted up his nostrils. A fresh wind—free of dust—blew in his face. Where was Nate? Someone had moved his body and covered him with a blanket. Gavin stumbled to the body and dropped to his knees. He peeled back the edge of the covering.

"Noooo!"

Gavin woke, startled to find himself standing next to the motel bed. He touched his naked chest and the heat radiating off his body burned his palm. He grabbed his keys and bolted outside to his truck. Once he started the engine, he blasted the air conditioner at his face. In less than a minute Gavin went from sweltering to shivering. His teeth chattered and his fingernails turned blue.

He sat in his truck, mesmerized by the blinking sign above the office of the Coral Motel in El Paso, Texas. Never before had the nightmare ended with Dixie's lifeless eyes staring up at Gavin.

God help him if he ever had the same dream again.

"YOU SHOULD HAVE STAYED in the army, Tucker. The more you ride, the worse you get." Chuckles followed the barb.

So much for the cowboy camaraderie Gavin had hoped to find on the rodeo circuit when he'd left the army. Ignoring the jeers of his competitors, he limped through the cowboy ready area of the Eldorado Arena in Eldorado, Oklahoma. He couldn't very well deny Trevor Mandela's accusation, mainly because it was dead-on. Gavin collected his gear and left the building.

He stood in the parking lot, staring at the sea of vehicles and livestock rigs. Where had he parked the truck? He dug his keys from his pocket and started walking, the light dusting of snow crunching beneath his boots. He pushed the panic button on the fob every few feet as he meandered through the rows. When he reached the middle of the lot a horn went off and he spotted the pickup's flashing headlights. He hit the panic button again to disengage the alarm. Once he stowed his bag in the backseat he hopped inside the cab and revved the engine. What now?

Today was November 4—the day he and Dixie were supposed to get married. Instead, he'd gotten his butt kicked at another rodeo and now he had nowhere to go.

If a bruised backside and a breaking heart weren't bad enough, he no longer enjoyed busting broncs. The adrenaline rush he'd come to depend on for his survival had deserted him, leaving him a hollow shell of a man—and it was all Dixie's fault. He'd fallen in love with a woman who was better off without him.

He glanced at the rearview mirror and grimaced. His cheeks were sunken hollows in his face and the dark circles beneath his eyes made him resemble a villain not America's hero—all because of a recurring nightmare. Since the last time he'd seen Dixie he'd resorted to sleeping in snatches, fearing if he rested too long the nightmare would hold him prisoner.

You can't go on like this.

Lack of sleep was affecting his physical strength and his will to win. What was the point anymore?

He fished his phone from his pocket and checked for messages. None. When he'd purchased a new cell phone a while back he should have changed the number, but he hadn't the courage to make a clean break from Dixie. Maybe he should have because Dixie's silence convinced him that she'd moved on with her life.

If only he could find a way to do the same.

The holidays were breathing down Gavin's neck. He doubted he could come up with a plausible excuse for not spending them with his mother. When he'd phoned to inform her of Dixie's miscarriage and the wedding being called off, she'd insisted he drive up and spend some time with her. He'd politely declined the invitation. Sympathy from his mother would weaken his resolve to put Dixie and the baby behind him.

That's the coward's way out.

Running was easier than coming to terms with the past—a process he wasn't sure he'd survive.

Don't run. Face your demons—for Dixie.

Dixie had carved a place for herself in Gavin's heart and he hadn't realized until she'd lost the baby how much she'd come to mean to him. In a short time she'd become his reason for living and had taught him to find joy in the little things life offered. Dixie had given him hope that one day he might be absolved for the role he'd played in Nate's death.

Dixie had become his everything.

Now she's your nothing.

Go see her. Tell her you want—no need—her in your life.

Gavin closed his eyes and envisioned himself barreling up the dirt drive to the farm, honking the horn. Dixie would step from the house wearing a welcoming smile. The only way that scenario would come to life was if he got help. He'd used Dixie, the baby, then the impending wedding as excuses to avoid confronting the demons that had followed him home from war.

The baby wasn't in the picture, the wedding had been called off and Dixie deserved better than sharing her life with a man and his tormented soul. The only way he could return to Stagecoach and ask Dixie to spend the rest of her life with him was if he sought professional help.

You have nothing to lose.

Nothing—save the woman who'd come to mean everything to him.

And Dixie was worth fighting for.

Chapter Fifteen

The third week in November Dixie pulled into the apartment complex and parked in a visitor's spot. After chasing empty leads on the rodeo circuit, she was tired and grumpy and darn weary of hauling her heavy broken heart around with her. If Sylvia Tucker didn't know her son's whereabouts then Dixie was calling it quits and returning to Stagecoach.

An urgency she hadn't felt before now accompanied her as she strolled along the sidewalk of the first building. When she spotted apartment 112, she took a fortifying breath and rang the bell. The door opened and a loud woof sounded in the background.

"May I help you?"

"I hope so." Dixie flashed a weak smile. "Are you Sylvia Tucker?"

"Yes, I am. Who are you?"

"Dixie Cash, ma'am." She paused not knowing if she should add "the girl your son got pregnant. The girl who miscarried your son's baby. The girl who's in love with your son and doesn't know how she'll live without him."

The door opened wider and Gavin's mother waved her inside. Dixie followed her into the kitchen. "Sit down. I was just about to make tea."

Tea would be welcome. "Thank you, Ms.—"

"Call me Sylvia." She smiled as she filled the teapot at the sink. "I was hoping you'd show up here."

Dixie's eyes widened. "You were?"

Sylvia set the kettle on the stove and joined Dixie at the table. She squeezed Dixie's hand. "I'm sorry about the baby, honey."

The heartfelt words touched Dixie. "Thank you."

"My son needs you."

And I need him. "Do you know where Gavin is?"

"He's at his therapy appointment."

Therapy? "Did he injure himself in a rodeo?"

"Not that kind of therapy." The kettle whistled and Sylvia spent the next few minutes preparing the tea. When she sat down again, she said, "Gavin's seeing a psychologist."

"For what?" Had losing the baby affected him more than Dixie believed?

"It's not my place to tell, honey."

"I need to talk to him." *I need to tell him I love him.*

Sylvia's teeth worried her lower lip as if uncertain about confiding in Dixie. Finally she rose from the table and scribbled on a notepad by the phone. She tore off the paper and held it out. "His appointment ends in thirty minutes. If you hurry, you could wait for him outside the building."

Dixie grabbed the address and rushed to the door. "Thank you, Sylvia," she called over her shoulder. As soon as Dixie got in the truck, she input the address in the GPS system Johnny had insisted she use when she'd left to search for Gavin. The medical building was less than ten miles away.

The Phoenix freeways were busy and full of crazy drivers, forcing Dixie to concentrate on the road and not allow her thoughts to wander to Gavin. The GPS signaled her to exit the freeway and the medical building was only a mile up the street. She pulled into the parking lot and drove past the various entrances, reading the numbers etched into the glass on the doors. When she spotted 130B she pulled into a space nearby and waited.

She didn't have to wait long. Gavin emerged from the building, pausing to put on his sunglasses. Dixie honked the horn and he froze, his gaze scanning the lot. She got out of the truck. Like cement blocks, her feet dragged across the pavement as she walked toward him. She knew the instant he spotted her—his shoulders stiffened and he glanced along the sidewalk as if seeking an escape route. Dixie's heart sank. She stopped short of the sidewalk and swallowed hard. *Please be happy to see me, Gavin.*

"I've been looking all over for you," she said. No sense pretending she'd just happened to be in the neighborhood.

"How did you find out I was here?"

"Your mother. She gave me the address."

His mouth pressed into a thin line.

"I need to tell you something, Gavin."

Gaze fastened to the pavement, he removed his sunglasses and pinched the bridge of his nose. When he finally lifted his head, the wounded look in his eyes broke Dixie's heart. "Don't say anything." He shook his head. "Just…don't. Please."

She wasn't letting him off the hook that easy. "I love you, Gavin. I didn't want to admit it, but I began falling for you the night we went to your motel room after the Boot Hill Rodeo."

"You can't." He shook his head and fisted his hands.

"Can't what?"

"Love me."

If she could just touch him… Show him the depth of her feelings… "Why can't I love you?"

"I'm not…" He walked away then stopped and faced her. "I'm not well."

"What do you mean?"

"I'm sick, Dixie." He punctuated the remark by poking himself in the head.

"Are you trying to scare me away?"

He took her by the arm and escorted her to her pickup where he opened the door and all but shoved her into the driver's seat. Once he shut the door, his shoulders relaxed as if relieved to have a barrier between them.

"I've been diagnosed with PTSD," he said. "That should damn well scare you."

Dixie had heard stories of soldiers returning from war who struggled with the medical condition. Things didn't always end well for many of them. The thought of Gavin suffering alone made her heart physically ache. "But you're working on getting better." She motioned at the door to the medical office.

"Being with you made me feel better so I ignored my problems and convinced myself that you could heal me." He rubbed a hand over his exhausted face. "That wasn't fair to you."

"I'm glad you're getting professional help, but you don't have to push me away."

"There's no cure for PTSD, Dixie."

"So this is it? You're going to take the coward's way out and use your PTSD as an excuse to run from what we have?"

The muscle along his jaw bunched—the only signal that her words had angered him. "You can learn to manage your symptoms, Gavin. It doesn't have to keep you from living the life you deserve."

"Easier said than done."

"Let me help you."

"No." He raised his hands as if warding her off. "I can't trust myself not to hurt you."

"But you've never lost control before."

"I have nightmares, Dixie. Horrible nightmares and they're becoming more intense."

"Why?"

"My shrink thinks it's because of the baby and—" He looked away. "You."

Dixie understood losing the baby might cause a relapse, but...*her?* "What have I done to distress you? Tell me and I'll stop doing it."

"You've done nothing wrong." He slammed his fist against his chest. "Not a damn thing except make me love you."

"You love me?" Tears leaked from her eyes and her heart swelled with hope.

"I love you enough to know that I'm not the right guy for you."

"But—"

"Just go, Dixie."

"I'll wait for you."

"No. You have to move on with your life."

"Well, that presents a problem, Gavin. I can't and I won't get on with my life without you." Dixie paused, giving him a chance to speak. When he remained silent she grasped at straws. "The love I feel for you isn't something I can turn on and off like a faucet. My love won't fade away just because we're not together."

He stared into the distance and Dixie felt her hope slipping away.

"Can't you find enough strength inside you for one more battle, Gavin? For me? For us?"

Please, Gavin. Please fight for me because without you... She couldn't finish the thought. She started the truck and shifted into Reverse. "Take as long as you need to get better, because I'm not going anywhere." Dixie backed out of the spot. Before leaving the medical plaza she checked the rearview mirror. Gavin watched her, the desolate expression on his face tearing her apart.

Find your way back to me, Gavin.

Late that night Dixie pulled into the farm and Johnny met her at the door. "You look like hell. What happened?"

She waltzed past him into the kitchen, then sank onto a chair at the table. "I found Gavin."

Johnny poured her a cup of coffee. "Where was he?"

"In Phoenix at his mother's place."

"Well...?"

"He's seeing a psychologist for PTSD."

"That's rough."

"I told him it didn't matter. That I still loved him." The tears she'd held inside her during the drive back from Phoenix threatened to escape. "Gavin doesn't want us to be together unless he can trust himself not to lose control."

"Does he love you?"

"Yes." But he'd made loving her sound as if it tortured his soul. "He told me to move on with my life and not wait for him."

"Is that what you plan to do?"

"Shoot, no. I'm staying right here until he comes to his senses and realizes that I'm the key to finding the peace he's searching for."

Johnny grinned. "Now, that's the spirited girl Grandma Ada raised."

His words made Dixie smile. "I better get to bed if I'm going into the store early tomorrow."

"Speaking of the store, you were right," Johnny said.

"Right about what?"

"Porter damn near sold out your inventory."

"Looks like I'll be putting in longer hours." She shuffled from the room but stopped when Johnny called after her.

"Dixie?"

"What?"

"I'll talk to Gavin if you want me to."

"Thanks but this is something Gavin has to work through on his own." Dixie just hoped that knowing she waited for him—that she wasn't giving up on their love—was enough to help Gavin find his way back to her.

CHRISTMAS CAME AND WENT as did New Year's and still no word from Gavin—just a holiday card from his mother informing Dixie that he'd continued to see his therapist and was working a part-time construction job. Tomorrow was February 1—almost twelve weeks had passed since Dixie had confronted Gavin outside his therapist's office.

Several times a day she picked up her phone intent on calling him just to hear his voice. It was doubly hard, like now—during the long ride home after a day at the gift shop—to resist reminding Gavin that she was still waiting. Her resolve to remain strong and give him the space he needed weakened with each passing day. The excitement of running her own business had waned in the wake of Gavin's absence. Even the sunrise and sunset had lost its glow.

Dixie took the turn off to the farm, glad tomorrow

was Monday and the gift shop was closed. She'd use the day to catch up on housework and laundry and think about Gavin and how much she missed him. She slowed the truck as she drove into the yard and parked by the barn. Halfway to the house she stopped, her heart pounding.

Gavin's truck sat among her brother's vehicles.

He came home.

Switching directions, she walked over to Gavin's pickup and placed her hand on the hood. Cool to the touch. How long had he been here? How long did he intend to stay?

"Gavin?" she hollered when she stepped through the front door.

"He's not here," Buck's voice floated down the hallway.

Dixie hurried into the kitchen. Her brothers were playing cards at the kitchen table—what else was new. "Gavin's truck is parked outside." She stated the obvious. "Where is he?"

"Out back," Willie answered.

Out back comprised two hundred acres. "Can you narrow it down?"

Johnny cleared his throat and her brothers tossed their cards down and shuffled from the room.

"Oh, God. It's bad, isn't it?"

"I don't know, Dixie. When Gavin got here, he asked to speak with you."

"What'd you tell him?"

"That you were still in Yuma at the store." Johnny nodded to the door. "Go talk to him. He went to Addie's grave."

The blood drained from Dixie's face. "How long has he been out there?"

"Over two hours."

She stared at the back door until Johnny's hand on her arm broke her trance. "He needs you, Dixie."

She yearned to believe her brother, but what if Gavin only returned for answers about the baby? Maybe his therapist had sent him to learn if they'd had a daughter or a son.

"I'm a mess." She smoothed a hand over her hair.

Johnny spun her around and unraveled her braid. After detangling the strands, he spread her hair across her shoulders. "There. Now you're pretty."

"You'll be here when I get back?"

"We'll all be here," Buck said. Her brothers hovered in the doorway. They were pains in the ass, but Dixie felt blessed to have their support. She left the house and cut through the backyard, walking east into the rows of pecan trees. The family plot was hidden behind a rocky knoll.

The sun shone brightly. No clouds—only blue sky. Crystal-clear blue. The day looked like a million other Arizona days. Somehow it didn't seem right that the world went on undisturbed, unmarred and unchanged after Addie had passed on. At the very least her little girl deserved ominous clouds, booming thunder and gale-force winds—a storm to protest her passing. Dixie trudged on, too tired to shake her fist at the heavens.

The graveyard came into view and she slowed her steps. The small rectangle was enclosed by a three foot high iron gate, which Gavin had left open. The rusty hinges groaned in the breeze.

The closer Dixie drew to the plot the more strength each step required. Gavin knelt at the foot of Addie's grave—the mound so tiny he could easily reach out his hand and touch the heart-shaped marker Johnny had ordered for his niece. Fresh flowers lay beneath the head-stone—Gavin must have brought those.

She stepped past the gate, her gaze landing on her grandmother's grave. A breath of wind hit Dixie in the face—Grandma Ada giving her encouragement. Dixie sank to her knees beside Gavin. They knelt in silence for the longest time and then Gavin reached for her hand. She gripped his fingers as if they were a lifeline.

Tears she'd already cried for her daughter filled her eyes again and she sniffed. Gavin folded her in a hug and they cried together—his shoulders shaking and her tears dampening his shirt.

Dixie had no idea how long they held each other, but she was grateful that they were finally mourning for their daughter together.

"I wanted to know if we'd had a girl or a boy."

"She was so tiny, Gavin. So precious."

"Addie's with your grandmother now," he said.

"Grandma Ada will take good care of our daughter until we see her again."

The sun sunk lower in the sky, smearing the horizon with a warm pinkish-purple hue. "I'm sad we lost Addie, but..." Gavin swallowed hard.

"But what?"

His gaze returned to her face and eyes damp with moisture beseeched her. "I don't want to lose you, too."

She flung her arms around his neck and held him tightly. "I've waited forever to hear those words, Gavin."

"I love you, Dixie." His rough, callused hands clasped her face. "I've made progress with my thera-pist but the scars will never go away."

"Scars don't scare me, Gavin, but living without you does."

He brushed his lips across her forehead. "I don't

know what I did to deserve you. I tried like hell to walk away from you, but I couldn't."

"Gavin, I promise—"

He pressed a finger to her lips, silencing her. "I realized that I hurt more from not having you in my life than from all the pain and heartache I suffered in Afghanistan."

She hugged him tight. "I love all of you—the healed and the hurting."

"I'm going to need therapy for a long time."

"Doesn't matter. We're in this together for a lifetime."

"Be sure, Dixie. Once you're mine, I'll never let you go."

She caressed his cheek. "I've always been yours and there's nowhere I want to be except by your side."

"Will you marry me, Dixie?" His kiss was a gentle caress…soft, fleeting, a whisper of devotion, need and desire.

"Yes, I'll marry you." Dixie deepened the kiss, wanting there to be no doubt in Gavin's mind that she'd stand by his side and love him no matter what his struggles were.

When the kiss ended, Gavin reached into his jeans pocket and removed a jeweler's box. "This time I'm doing it, right."

"You already gave me a ring." Dixie hadn't taken off the ring since Gavin had slipped it on her finger months ago.

"You deserve better than someone's castoff." He opened the ring box to reveal a one-carat marquise diamond.

She gasped. "Gavin…it's stunning." Good Lord, this

must have cost a fortune. "It's too expensive." She shook her head. "I can't accept it."

Ignoring her protests, he removed the pawn-shop ring from her finger and slid the new diamond on. "I want everyone to know you're mine, Dixie." He kissed her once again and this time when they came up for air, Gavin stood and helped Dixie to her feet. "Where are we going to live?"

"Right here on the farm."

"There are six other men in that house."

"My grandmother left the farm to me, Gavin. It's mine. My brothers are allowed to live here until they reach the age of thirty-five or get married—whichever comes first."

Gavin's gaze settled on the heart-shaped headstone. "I like the idea of being close to Addie." He grasped Dixie's hand. "Let's go tell your brothers to start looking for wives or apartments."

"No need," Dixie said. "They're building a bunk-house behind the barn."

"What for?"

"To sleep in after we're married."

"You were that sure I'd come back for you?"

"I never doubted for a minute."

Hand in hand they walked back to the house and for the first time since her miscarriage, Dixie was able to draw a deep breath without her chest hurting. "I'd planned to give you until the beginning of the summer to come to your senses," she said.

"Or what?"

"Or I'd have driven up to Phoenix and fetched you home."

"Like a stray dog, eh?" Gavin's booming laughter

echoed through the pecan grove and drew Dixie's brothers onto the back porch.

They stopped in the yard and Gavin pulled her close, his mouth hovering over hers. "You're my one and only, Dixie. I love you."

"I guess this means we'd better finish the bunkhouse sooner rather than later," Willie said.

"No one's moving out of this house until they tie the knot." Johnny sent Gavin a stern look.

Dixie and Gavin approached the porch. "Porter," Dixie said. "You'd better contact Reverend Thomas right away." Her brother dashed into the house.

"This isn't a joke, is it, Dixie?" Willie asked.

She held up her ring finger and smiled.

Willie let out a low whistle. "Now, that's a proper engagement ring."

Johnny descended the steps and stopped in front of Gavin. "This better be for real, Tucker, or you'll have me and my brothers to answer to."

"It's for real, Johnny." Gavin smiled at Dixie. "I love your sister and I'll do everything in my power to make her happy." He swooped in for another kiss but stopped when the porch door banged against the side of the house.

"Wait!" Porter hollered. "No more kissing. Reverend Thomas said he'd marry Dixie and Gavin right now."

"How'd you get him to agree to officiate a wedding on such short notice?" Buck asked.

"I said if he didn't, Johnny was getting out the shotgun."

"You're such a drama queen, Porter," Merle said.

"What about your mother?" Dixie asked Gavin. He was Sylvia Tucker's only child and Dixie assumed she'd want to be present when her son married.

"My mother wants me to be happy, Dixie. And marrying you…right now…makes me happy."

Willie let out a whoop and leaped off the porch. "Let's get going!"

"Wait. Give me ten minutes." Dixie raced into the house and up to her bedroom where she pulled out the plastic bin from beneath the bed. She removed her grandmother's silk wedding dress and spread it across the mattress. With loving hands she smoothed the wrinkles and then searched through the closet for the cream-colored heels she'd purchased three years ago but had never worn because they pinched her toes. Next, she opened her jewelry box and took out her grandmother's pearl necklace and matching earrings. She raised the bedroom window and hollered, "Conway! Get up here now!"

While she waited for her brother, she put on her nicest bra and panty set and slipped into the wedding gown just as the bedroom door flung open.

"What's the matter?" Conway panted.

"Help me button this." She presented her back and the double row of pearl buttons.

"My fingers are too clumsy." Conway cursed under his breath.

"You're the one who wanted a big shindig, be happy I'm wearing a wedding gown."

Conway grumbled but finished the job. He spun her around. "Did grandma have a veil?"

"No."

"Fix your hair. It's a mess." He handed her the hairbrush from the top of her dresser. Dixie gathered the long strands and pinned them to her head in a messy bob.

"That'll do." Conway kissed her cheek.

Arm in arm they walked through the house. When they stepped outside Gavin's slow, sexy smile made promises she intended to hold him accountable for later that evening.

"You look beautiful," he said.

"Wait. The camera." Conway went back into the house and came out a second later. "Okay. We're ready."

Johnny grabbed Gavin's arm. "You're riding with me…in case you get cold feet."

"I'll take the bride." Conway snagged Dixie's hand and tugged her across the yard to Willie's pickup. Porter jumped in with them while Buck and Merle went in Johnny's truck.

Maybe it was a good thing Johnny was escorting Gavin to the chapel, because as soon as Gavin realized he wasn't just marrying Dixie but also her six crazy brothers, he really might make a run for it.

As the pickups sped down the dirt road, Dixie swiveled in her seat and stared out the rear window at Johnny's truck. Gavin was grinning from ear to ear.

Dixie lifted her smile to the heavens. *Thank you for bringing Gavin into my life, Grandma Ada. He not only made your dream come true, but he made mine, too.*

* * * * *

COMING NEXT MONTH from Harlequin®
American Romance®
AVAILABLE SEPTEMBER 4, 2012

#1417 DUKE: DEPUTY COWBOY
Harts of the Rodeo
Roz Denny Fox
Duke Adams is a solid, dependable lawman, great with kids and a champion bull rider. He'd be perfect—except Angie Barrington can't stand rodeo cowboys....

#1418 THE COWBOY SOLDIER'S SONS
Callahan Cowboys
Tina Leonard
Retired from military service, Shaman Phillips comes to Tempest, New Mexico, to find peace. The last thing he expects to find is a blonde bombshell who just might be the key to his redemption.

#1419 RESCUED BY A RANGER
Hill Country Heroes
Tanya Michaels
Hiding out in the Texas Hill Country, single mother Alex Hunt is living a lie. But can she keep her secrets from the irresistible lawman next door?

#1420 THE M.D.'S SECRET DAUGHTER
Safe Harbor Medical
Jacqueline Diamond
Eight years ago, after Dr. Zack Sargent betrayed her trust, Jan Garcia broke their engagement and moved away...never telling him she kept the child she was supposed to give up for adoption.

REQUEST YOUR FREE BOOKS!
2 FREE NOVELS PLUS 2 FREE GIFTS!

 Harlequin®

LOVE, HOME & HAPPINESS

YES! Please send me 2 FREE Harlequin® American Romance® novels and my 2 FREE gifts (gifts are worth about $10). After receiving them, if I don't wish to receive any more books, I can return the shipping statement marked "cancel." If I don't cancel, I will receive 4 brand-new novels every month and be billed just $4.49 per book in the U.S. or $5.24 per book in Canada. That's a saving of at least 14% off the cover price! It's quite a bargain! Shipping and handling is just 50¢ per book in the U.S. and 75¢ per book in Canada.* I understand that accepting the 2 free books and gifts places me under no obligation to buy anything. I can always return a shipment and cancel at any time. Even if I never buy another book, the two free books and gifts are mine to keep forever.

154/354 HDN FEP2

Name _____ (PLEASE PRINT) _____

Address _____ Apt. # _____

City _____ State/Prov. _____ Zip/Postal Code _____

Signature (if under 18, a parent or guardian must sign)

Mail to the **Reader Service:**
IN U.S.A.: P.O. Box 1867, Buffalo, NY 14240-1867
IN CANADA: P.O. Box 609, Fort Erie, Ontario L2A 5X3

Not valid for current subscribers to Harlequin American Romance books.

Want to try two free books from another line?
Call 1-800-873-8635 or visit www.ReaderService.com.

* Terms and prices subject to change without notice. Prices do not include applicable taxes. Sales tax applicable in N.Y. Canadian residents will be charged applicable taxes. Offer not valid in Quebec. This offer is limited to one order per household. All orders subject to credit approval. Credit or debit balances in a customer's account(s) may be offset by any other outstanding balance owed by or to the customer. Please allow 4 to 6 weeks for delivery. Offer available while quantities last.

Your Privacy—The Reader Service is committed to protecting your privacy. Our Privacy Policy is available online at www.ReaderService.com or upon request from the Reader Service.

We make a portion of our mailing list available to reputable third parties that offer products we believe may interest you. If you prefer that we not exchange your name with third parties, or if you wish to clarify or modify your communication preferences, please visit us at www.ReaderService.com/consumerchoice or write to us at Reader Service Preference Service, P.O. Box 9062, Buffalo, NY 14269. Include your complete name and address.

HAR11B

Welcome to the Texas Hill Country! In the third book in Tanya Michaels's series HILL COUNTRY HEROES, *a desperate mother is in hiding with her little girl. The last thing she needs is her nosy Texas Ranger neighbor getting friendly....*

Alex raised her gaze, starting to say something, but then she froze like a possum in oncoming headlights.

"Mrs. Hunt? Everything okay?"

She eyed the encircled silver star pinned to his denim button-down shirt. He'd been working this morning and hadn't bothered to remove the badge. "Interesting symbol," she said slowly.

"Represents the Texas Rangers."

"L-like the baseball team?"

"No, ma'am. Like the law enforcement agency." Maybe that would make her feel safer about her temporary new surroundings. He jerked his thumb toward his house. "You have a bona fide lawman living right next door."

Beneath the freckles, her face went whiter than his hat. "Really? That's…" She gave herself a quick shake. "Come on, Belle. Inside now. Before, um, before that mud stains."

"Okay." Belle hung her head but rallied long enough to add, "Bye-bye, Mister Zane. I hope I get to pet Dolly again soon."

From Alex's behavior, Zane had a suspicion they wouldn't be getting together for neighborly potluck dinners anytime in the near future. Instead of commenting on the kid's likelihood of seeing Dolly again, he waved. "Bye, Belle. Stay fabulous."

She beamed. "I will!"

Then mother and daughter disappeared into the house, the front door banging shut behind them.

"Is there something about me," he asked Dolly, "that makes females want to slam doors?"

The only response he got from the dog was an impatient tug on her leash. "Right. I promised you a walk." They started again down the sidewalk, but he found himself periodically glancing over his shoulder and pondering his new neighbors. Cute kid, but she seemed like a handful. And Alex Hunt, once she'd calmed from her mama-bear fury, was perhaps the most skittish woman he'd ever met. If she were a horse, she'd have to wear blinders to keep from jumping at her own shadow. Zane wondered if there was a Mr. Hunt in the picture.

Be sure to look for RESCUED BY A RANGER
by Tanya Michaels in September 2012 from
Harlequin® American Romance®!

SPECIAL EDITION

Life, Love and Family

NEW YORK TIMES BESTSELLING AUTHOR

KATHLEEN EAGLE

brings readers a story of a cowboy's return home

Ethan Wolf Track is a true cowboy—rugged, wild and commitment-free. He's returned home to South Dakota to rebuild his life, and he'll start by competing in Mustang Sally's Wild Horse Training Competition.... But TV reporter Bella Primeaux is on the hunt for a different kind of prize, and she'll do whatever it takes to uncover the truth.

THE PRODIGAL COWBOY

Available September 2012 wherever books are sold!